Man-Killers of the Air

SELECTED FICTION WORKS BY L. RON HUBBARD

FANTASY
The Case of the Friendly Corpse
Death's Deputy
Fear
The Ghoul
The Indigestible Triton
Slaves of Sleep & The Masters of Sleep
Typewriter in the Sky
The Ultimate Adventure

SCIENCE FICTION
Battlefield Earth
The Conquest of Space
The End Is Not Yet
Final Blackout
The Kilkenny Cats
The Kingslayer
The Mission Earth Dekalogy*
Ole Doc Methuselah
To the Stars

ADVENTURE
The Hell Job series

WESTERN
Buckskin Brigades
Empty Saddles
Guns of Mark Jardine
Hot Lead Payoff

A full list of L. Ron Hubbard's
novellas and short stories is provided at the back.

*Dekalogy—a group of ten volumes

L. RON HUBBARD

Man-Killers
of the Air

Published by
Galaxy Press, LLC
7051 Hollywood Boulevard, Suite 200
Hollywood, CA 90028

© 2008 L. Ron Hubbard Library. All Rights Reserved.

Any unauthorized copying, translation, duplication, importation or distribution, in whole or in part, by any means, including electronic copying, storage or transmission, is a violation of applicable laws.

Mission Earth is a trademark owned by L. Ron Hubbard Library and is used with permission. *Battlefield Earth* is a trademark owned by Author Services, Inc. and is used with permission.

Horsemen illustration from *Western Story Magazine* is © and ™ Condé Nast Publications and is used with their permission. Fantasy, Far-Flung Adventure and Science Fiction illustrations: *Unknown* and *Astounding Science Fiction* copyright © by Street & Smith Publications, Inc. Reprinted with permission of Penny Publications, LLC. Story Preview cover art and illustration: *Argosy Magazine* is © 1936 Argosy Communications, Inc. All Rights Reserved.
Reprinted with permission from Argosy Communications, Inc.

Printed in the United States of America.

ISBN-10 1-59212-291-4
ISBN-13 978-1-59212-291-2

Library of Congress Control Number: 2007903624

Contents

Foreword	vii
Man-Killers of the Air	1
Story Preview: Sabotage in the Sky	83
Glossary	91
L. Ron Hubbard in the Golden Age of Pulp Fiction	97
The Stories from the Golden Age	109

FOREWORD

Stories from Pulp Fiction's Golden Age

AND it *was* a golden age. The 1930s and 1940s were a vibrant, seminal time for a gigantic audience of eager readers, probably the largest per capita audience of readers in American history. The magazine racks were chock-full of publications with ragged trims, garish cover art, cheap brown pulp paper, low cover prices—and the most excitement you could hold in your hands.

"Pulp" magazines, named for their rough-cut, pulpwood paper, were a vehicle for more amazing tales than Scheherazade could have told in a million and one nights. Set apart from higher-class "slick" magazines, printed on fancy glossy paper with quality artwork and superior production values, the pulps were for the "rest of us," adventure story after adventure story for people who liked to *read*. Pulp fiction authors were no-holds-barred entertainers—real storytellers. They were more interested in a thrilling plot twist, a horrific villain or a white-knuckle adventure than they were in lavish prose or convoluted metaphors.

The sheer volume of tales released during this wondrous golden age remains unmatched in any other period of literary history—hundreds of thousands of published stories in over nine hundred different magazines. Some titles lasted only an

• FOREWORD •

issue or two; many magazines succumbed to paper shortages during World War II, while others endured for decades yet. Pulp fiction remains as a treasure trove of stories you can read, stories you can love, stories you can remember. The stories were driven by plot and character, with grand heroes, terrible villains, beautiful damsels (often in distress), diabolical plots, amazing places, breathless romances. The readers wanted to be taken beyond the mundane, to live adventures far removed from their ordinary lives—and the pulps rarely failed to deliver.

In that regard, pulp fiction stands in the tradition of all memorable literature. For as history has shown, good stories are much more than fancy prose. William Shakespeare, Charles Dickens, Jules Verne, Alexandre Dumas—many of the greatest literary figures wrote their fiction for the readers, not simply literary colleagues and academic admirers. And writers for pulp magazines were no exception. These publications reached an audience that dwarfed the circulations of today's short story magazines. Issues of the pulps were scooped up and read by over thirty million avid readers each month.

Because pulp fiction writers were often paid no more than a cent a word, they had to become prolific or starve. They also had to write aggressively. As Richard Kyle, publisher and editor of *Argosy*, the first and most long-lived of the pulps, so pointedly explained: "The pulp magazine writers, the best of them, worked for markets that did not write for critics or attempt to satisfy timid advertisers. Not having to answer to anyone other than their readers, they wrote about human

• FOREWORD •

beings on the edges of the unknown, in those new lands the future would explore. They wrote for what we would become, not for what we had already been."

Some of the more lasting names that graced the pulps include H. P. Lovecraft, Edgar Rice Burroughs, Robert E. Howard, Max Brand, Louis L'Amour, Elmore Leonard, Dashiell Hammett, Raymond Chandler, Erle Stanley Gardner, John D. MacDonald, Ray Bradbury, Isaac Asimov, Robert Heinlein—and, of course, L. Ron Hubbard.

In a word, he was among the most prolific and popular writers of the era. He was also the most enduring—hence this series—and certainly among the most legendary. It all began only months after he first tried his hand at fiction, with L. Ron Hubbard tales appearing in *Thrilling Adventures, Argosy, Five-Novels Monthly, Detective Fiction Weekly, Top-Notch, Texas Ranger, War Birds, Western Stories,* even *Romantic Range.* He could write on any subject, in any genre, from jungle explorers to deep-sea divers, from G-men and gangsters, cowboys and flying aces to mountain climbers, hard-boiled detectives and spies. But he really began to shine when he turned his talent to science fiction and fantasy of which he authored nearly fifty novels or novelettes to forever change the shape of those genres.

Following in the tradition of such famed authors as Herman Melville, Mark Twain, Jack London and Ernest Hemingway, Ron Hubbard actually lived adventures that his own characters would have admired—as an ethnologist among primitive tribes, as prospector and engineer in hostile climes, as a captain of vessels on four oceans. He even wrote a series of articles for *Argosy*, called "Hell Job," in which he lived and told of the most dangerous professions a man could put his hand to.

Finally, and just for good measure, he was also an accomplished photographer, artist, filmmaker, musician and educator. But he was first and foremost a *writer*, and that's the L. Ron Hubbard we come to know through the pages of this volume.

This library of Stories from the Golden Age presents the best of L. Ron Hubbard's fiction from the heyday of storytelling, the Golden Age of the pulp magazines. In these eighty volumes, readers are treated to a full banquet of 153 stories, a kaleidoscope of tales representing every imaginable genre: science fiction, fantasy, western, mystery, thriller, horror, even romance—action of all kinds and in all places.

Because the pulps themselves were printed on such inexpensive paper with high acid content, issues were not meant to endure. As the years go by, the original issues of every pulp from *Argosy* through *Zeppelin Stories* continue crumbling into brittle, brown dust. This library preserves the L. Ron Hubbard tales from that era, presented with a distinctive look that brings back the nostalgic flavor of those times.

L. Ron Hubbard's Stories from the Golden Age has something for every taste, every reader. These tales will return you to a time when fiction was good clean entertainment and

• FOREWORD •

the most fun a kid could have on a rainy afternoon or the best thing an adult could enjoy after a long day at work.

Pick up a volume, and remember what reading is supposed to be all about. Remember curling up with a *great story*.

—Kevin J. Anderson

KEVIN J. ANDERSON *is the author of more than ninety critically acclaimed works of speculative fiction, including* The Saga of Seven Suns, *the continuation of the Dune Chronicles with Brian Herbert, and his* New York Times *bestselling novelization of L. Ron Hubbard's* Ai! Pedrito!

Man-Killers of the Air

CHAPTER ONE

A Dangerous Bet

LESS than a hundred years ago, a cannonball traveled about sixty miles an hour when it was going fast. Smoke Burnham, with his throttle a quarter back, was sliding down the sky at four times the rate of a cannonball. And he still found time to glance overboard at the ground—where people looked like pepper strewn on wrapping paper—and say with great bitterness, "Damn it! He's done it again!"

The single-winged, stubby racing ship was mostly engine with fins attached. And yet it had two cockpits. It was all metal, and when the sun struck it, people had red spots before their eyes for hours after.

Smoke Burnham's remarks referred to Alex Montague, the man who could sell the Brooklyn Bridge five times in one afternoon and still find enough leisure to promote a new flying field.

This test flight—a mere jaunt of a thousand miles—had been strictly on the QT four hours before, but now it looked as though the whole world had heard of it and had turned out to see Smoke Burnham land the new two-seater pursuit which Smoke's plant had recently developed.

Smoke didn't mind the crowd for the crowd's sake. Smoke knew the value of publicity—Montague had taught him that. But Smoke did hate to be driven away from his own field.

After all, when people get tangled in prop and landing gear, it's liable to be embarrassing all the way around.

Umpteen hundred horses up front were snorting in mighty discord. The retracted landing wheels whistled shrilly as the air caught them in the process of being lowered. People stared worshipfully upward, for this was Smoke Burnham, *the* Smoke Burnham. Their ears would have burned had they heard what he called them.

At one time in his career, Smoke Burnham had hated to land on a crowded field because the people immediately rushed in and tore him apart. He had taken care of that now.

A velvety nose was peering out of the gunner's cockpit. Sleek dun-colored ears. Baleful yellow eyes which looked out at the cloudless sky and racing ground through a pair of specially tailored goggles.

This was Patty, the cheetah. An admirer Smoke had never seen had given him this hunting leopard straight from India. Smoke's friends had wondered what use a racing pilot might have for a cheetah. They left it to Montague to find out. Crowds weren't so eager when Patty purred softly and rubbed against Smoke's whipcords. There is something about a cheetah . . .

Smoke dived down at the field. His French cavalry glove came back on the stick. His grease-splattered helmet jutted over the side.

"Damn it!" he bellowed as he shot over the field. "Get off the runway!"

It is unlikely that they heard him, but the police knew

what he meant. In a moment the runway began to lighten in color, and when Smoke had spurred his charging mount around into the wind, he nosed down for a swift, clean landing.

As usual, they ran at him like so many potential assassins. Smoke hastily reached into the rear cockpit and hauled out Patty. A hundred-odd pounds of cheetah bounced lightly on the concrete, immediately brought to a halt by the leash.

Smiling with chapped lips, Smoke Burnham hopped down. Patty rubbed against him and the crowd halted a dozen feet back. They grinned and pointed, and told each other that this was Burnham, *the* Burnham, and that that was the Mystery Ship. Camera shutters rattled like machine-gun fire. Notebooks were waved. Smoke Burnham grinned, and Patty purred, and everyone appeared to be very happy.

And they were until Smoke spotted Paul Harrison Girard.

Smoke's grin faded a little and then came back, but his blue eyes were no longer smiling. His hard, wiry body was taut, and the hand on the cheetah's leash whitened along the knuckles.

He sauntered toward Girard, and Patty effectually cleared the way by smiling at one and all indiscriminately.

Smoke's face was mostly black, except where his goggles had ringed his eyes. His even teeth were in startling contrast to the rest of his face, and the parachute-silk scarf, though a little gray, served to set off the burnt-cork illusion which had been handed back from the flying heels of the umpteen hundred horses.

Alex Montague rushed out and pumped Smoke's hand with

great fervor. Alex had a large, kind face, topped by dignified gray hair. His sport-cut clothes were worn with the air of a cutaway.

"Great stuff, Smoke!" roared Alex. "Great stuff! You beat your own record with that ship—beat it both ends from the middle—and I want to be the first one to—"

"Can it," said Smoke through a tight mouth. "They aren't listening. Congratulate me for them later."

"What's the matter?" cried Alex. "Didn't you beat—"

"Pipe down. There's Girard."

"Gir-Girard? Where?"

"Behind that last bunch on the apron. I guess we weren't fast enough, Alex."

"Oh, don't take it to heart," said Alex, in a more natural voice. "We've been sold out before. To hell with it, Smoke. You're a hero right now. Make the best of it."

"Go give them your line, Alex. I'm going to get this thing finished up right now and no later. I'm tired of playing with the fat shylock."

Smoke, following the cheetah, cleared his path to the front of the concrete hangar which bore his name in gold letters across the doors. Letters six feet high. That had been Alex's idea. Alex was always having ideas. Like that one about Girard. How Girard would give them backing and see them through. And now Girard—

"Hi, Smoke! Great going!"

"Attaboy, Smoke. We got it in the bag!"

"Look, there's Smoke Burnham!"

Smoke gave everyone a big grin and went on toward Girard.

Girard was standing with both feet solidly planted, both hands shoved into the pockets of a pure camel's-hair overcoat. Girard's face looked as though someone had started to mold it from soggy putty and had then become bored with the job.

Girard was a big man—knew it, said it and acted it. He could afford to be a big man. He was one of the greatest newspaper publishers in the United States, one of the greatest exponents of that fourth stage of the newspaper, yellow journalism. He had once tipped a waiter a thousand-dollar bill, and the next day he had fired a legman for being twenty-five cents over on his swindle sheet.

Girard was surrounded by his own men, but one never saw those. They were dressed plainly, looked plain, were plain, and always nodded eagerly, "YES!"

"Well, well, well!" rumbled Girard. "That was some record, my boy, some record! Hey, you over there with the movie camera, want my picture shaking Burnham's hand?"

The movie man started to comply and then saw the look Smoke Burnham gave him. "No," said Smoke. "We aren't waving any flags. Not today. And I'm not shaking hands with you, Girard, any day!"

Girard was startled. "But, my boy—"

"Save it," said Smoke. "Let's get ahead with our business. You came up here to make me fork over the dough you lent me. And you've got the sheriff right there behind you, so don't deny it. You're foreclosing on Burnham Aeronautical Company, but you don't want to do it until the crowd goes."

Patty looked at Girard and licked her feline lips. Girard stared at both pilot and cheetah.

"Who put you wise?" he demanded.

"I did, mister. You haven't got a lease on all the brains in this country. You want this new fight-plane so you can turn it over to the government."

"But how—"

"I know what you're up to. You've got an air defense campaign underway, Girard. You're saying that the Japs are about to fly across San Francisco and wipe us out with bombers. And you're saying via a hundred newspapers that we haven't a single plane to withstand that offense.

"And, furthermore, you've challenged anyone to produce such a plane."

"You'd better watch out!" cried Girard, as though he wielded a saber instead of a Malacca cane.

"And," rapped Smoke, "you're going to foreclose on me, take the plans of this ship, the ship itself, and turn it over to the Army. That's patriotism! That's honor! You jump your ad rates on the resulting circulation and clean up."

Girard still waved the cane. He might have struck Smoke, because there were plenty of men behind Girard. But the cheetah was still licking her lips, and Smoke's hand was loose on the leash.

Two fighters, identical with the one Smoke had just flown in, crouched in the hangar. Smoke pointed to them. "Those two ships are company property. The one I used today belongs to Melanie King. I gave her the bill of sale. Now go ahead and serve your papers."

The sheriff, at Girard's nod, stepped up, skirting Patty's

striking range. Although Patty had never struck anyone, people thought she did, and that was just as good.

Smoke began to smile and then to grin. The effect through the grime was ghastly, but he meant it.

"If you'll come inside," said Smoke, "I'll sign everything up and we'll all go have some lunch."

Girard's face was puzzled. Smoke Burnham had more records than Girard had newspapers. A story about Smoke was worth a hundred-thousand circulation jump. But that was no sign Smoke was an open book. Warily, Girard stepped into the hangar in Smoke's wake.

Smoke indicated some folding chairs at the back, "Sit yourself down, gentlemen. I haven't any cigars, but I see you've brought your own." He thrust a cigarette into his mouth at a climbing angle and lit up. Patty sat down in front of him, watching the curling blue wisps.

Girard, far from trusting Smoke, seated himself. It was all that he could do.

Smoke, still holding the burning match in spite of the mammoth sign: *No Smoking! Fire Hazard!* looked casually about him. Under the belly of the first pursuit ship there was a small puddle of gasoline, spilled at the last filling and not yet wholly evaporated.

Smoke flipped the burning match into the puddle.

A geyser of white flame shot up. A piece of cotton waste, soaked with oil, ignited with a crackling sound.

Girard jumped to his feet. "Fire! My God, *fire!*"

Smoke watched the flames engulf the shiny metal. A tongue

slapped out and sideswiped the other ship. The heat rose from seventy to two hundred in a space of seconds.

Girard's crowd charged toward the hangar's doors, shrieking. Patty bared her fangs and unsheathed her claws in fear. Acrid fumes leaped, black and greasy.

On the outside of the hangar the crowd surged, shouting advice, shouting prayers, shouting anything as long as they made noise.

Alex ran wildly about crying, "Anybody seen Burnham? Where's Smoke?"

Newspaper men were milling, bellowing, "Where's Girard? Mr. Girard's in there!"

The thickening smoke was heavy and hot, completely filling the hangar. It was thick enough to carve.

A staggering man came out of the flame-seared maw. He was lugging another man.

Alex cried, "It's Smoke!"

The reporters yelled, "There's Girard!"

Smoke, stumbling and coughing, dropped his burden and then fell flat on his face. With a glance, Alex saw that Smoke was still all in one piece and that Girard was breathing.

Alex suddenly confronted the reporters. "There you are, boys! Get those pictures! Get this story! There you are!"

"What happened?" demanded a pale-faced newshawk.

Alex waved his hands majestically. "Girard accidentally threw a lighted cigar into a gasoline can and then Smoke stayed behind, searching for him. Looking through all that flaming hell. Fumbling under the ships, around already burning chairs.

*A staggering man came out of the flame-seared maw.
He was lugging another man.*

He heard a sound like coughing and crept nearer, not letting himself retreat from the searing, scorching heat. And then he found Girard. He found Girard, gentlemen, at the risk of his own life! And there's Girard, safe and sound. But he would be but a blackened corpse if Smoke Burnham had not—"

Girard was sitting up. He saw the reporters running toward the phones. It was too late to stop them. And besides, circulation would soar instantly with those headlines. Money was in the making.

But that did not keep Girard from rolling closer to Smoke. The publisher's flame-stung face was the color of raw beef. His eyes were a sickly red.

"You win, Burnham. But I'll make you a bet. I'll bet this place rebuilt against that one last pursuit plane."

Smoke grinned and lit a cigarette, as though he had not had enough smoke as it was. Patty, licking scorched fur, watched him with adoring eyes.

"Okay," said Smoke. "What's the bet?"

"That you can't win my transcontinental derby next month."

Smoke nodded. "Do you recall the other contest before that?"

"Yes. You'll have to win that before you can get into the derby."

"Make it a place twice as big as this and you're on."

Girard smiled, circulation figures dancing before his eyes. "All right, Burnham. We'll have that put on paper."

CHAPTER TWO

Headliners Can't Go Hungry?

THE low-slung jet-black roadster curved to a stop beside the operations office, its brakes howling a raucous protest to the action. From the gleaming curves of metal stepped a girl. She was pensive, and her deep blue eyes glanced restlessly about in search of Smoke Burnham. She was dressed in a loose swagger coat which almost matched her eyes and beret. The car made her seem smaller than she really was.

Smoke Burnham was seated upon a discarded sawhorse. His yellow hair gleamed in the sun, combed straight back with only the smallest excuse for a part. His white-flanneled legs were crossed and his right foot swung slowly back and forth as he watched Patty complete her morning bath. Patty, with occasional glances at Smoke, as though to make certain that he was still with her, made a low, contented purring sound, liking the warm, yellow sun.

Alex Montague strode robustly forward and slapped his hand on Smoke's shoulder. "Well, boy, that was certainly great publicity. Great publicity! They plastered your face all over the editions. 'Smoke Saves Girard From Flames.' That's the stuff that takes the cake. Almost worth the loss of a quarter of a million of equipment." He jerked his thumb at the dead, blackened structure behind Smoke.

"Yeah," said Smoke. "Good publicity. You're fired, Alex."

Alex was startled out of his composure. "You mean you'll try to cap the climax by putting it out that I'm fired?"

"No. This isn't publicity, this is truth. We're finished, washed up. That's that."

Alex ran his hand through slightly gray hair, pleading, "Now listen, Smoke. You certainly— Listen, Smoke, what have I done?"

"Nothing. You haven't done anything I didn't like. I just can't pay you anymore, that's all."

"What's this?"

"I'm broke, get me? I spent the last dime on gas for the flight yesterday. The last dime. I'm broke and I can't pay you and we're through, and that's that."

"Aw, now listen, Smoke. Don't take it so hard. Can't—"

Smoke stood up, his face sad. "I meant it. Please don't make it any harder for me, Alex. That plant was all I had. Nothing saved up. Nothing in the war box for this. I've blown every dime into promoting that racer and pursuit plane out there for the Army. I can't pay you, and I'm through."

Alex scratched his head, screwing up his face, and stared out at the shiny all-metal ship. "That's bad, Smoke. But if you think I'm going to quit you—"

"Sure you're going to quit me. We've been together a long time and all that, but I pay my way as I go." Smoke turned his face back to Patty and sat down, again crossing his legs. "All I've got is that ship."

"But you can beat Girard at his game. You can win his race. He said he'd build you a factory twice the size of your last."

"Alex," said Smoke slowly, "you don't know Girard. He

worships a circulation sheet and lives in headlines. My death would make a good headline, increase circulation. Draw your own map."

"Sure, now, Smoke. Don't take it so hard. Girard wouldn't dare—"

"You know in your heart he would and will. He'll let me go just so far. I'll have a time getting into the prelims, and a hard fight even getting close to the final derby. And if I start to come out well enough in that, he'll take me for a ride. That's Girard, Alex—and you know it."

"Sure I do, Smoke, but—look, there comes Melanie. She's looking for you." Alex suddenly began to beam. "Listen. I've got it! Get a few thousand from Melanie and—"

Smoke whirled, glaring. "Do you think I'd take money from a woman? She's swell, Alex. I love her, but by God, I won't take money from her! She doesn't like to have me take these chances, and if she had any money in the game she'd see to it that I didn't fly anymore. And that—" He stopped with a sigh. "Don't tell her I'm broke, Alex. I don't want her to find out for a while. Let me keep her just a few more days. After that—"

Melanie King

Melanie King's cheerful voice and light footsteps came up to them. She was smiling as she looked at Smoke. Her hands were thrust deep into her pockets. It always made Smoke feel funny in his throat when she smiled at him that way.

"Hello, Alex," she said. "I hear you're getting a setup to whip Girard. Everything working out?"

Hastily, Alex said, "You bet it is. You bet it is. You bet—" He backed out of earshot.

"What's the matter with him?" she inquired.

"Cold or something," said Smoke, smiling. "Had to get to a hospital or a doctor, I forget just which. What are you doing out here so early?"

"Can't I get out here early if I want?" She seated herself on the other end of the sawhorse, laughing. "Or do I have to have my appointments with you?"

Smoke laughed with her. "But you've something up your sleeve, little lady. I can see it, feel it and I know it. What's today's business?"

"Oh, let's forget about today's business for the moment. I want to tell you how positively wonderful—"

"—I was when I dragged out fat Girard. Don't believe everything that Alex releases, Mel. First thing you know, you'll worry yourself all the time."

Her smile faded out of her eyes. "Perhaps . . . perhaps I do, Smoke."

"You'll be reading," continued Smoke, pretending not to notice, "how I spent my youth in Alaska—where I have never been—or how I—well, you might even read that I'm broke." He shot a quick, sidelong glance in her direction.

Gaily, she laughed at such an impossibility. "Not with all you've made from your records and contests!"

"In other words, a headliner can't get hungry. Maybe not, Mel. Now tell me why you came down here so early."

"Why, for the plane."

He stared at her blankly. "Plane? What plane?"

"The new pursuit plane you gave me. I'm going to have it taken up to the country house field. Father thought that I could keep it there. He said he'd get another man to teach me to fly it, if you didn't have the time."

It sank home to Smoke that she was serious. In truth he *had* given her the plane. Because he had three of them all alike, and because he wanted at least one out of Girard's reach. But he hadn't thought—

"But," said Smoke, "it's too fast for you to fly. You stay with slow ships and—"

"If you keep flying, I guess I can."

"Certainly, Mel. To be sure. But you see—it's a man-killer, that plane."

"Anything that travels over two-fifty an hour is a man-killer," she countered. "But if I want to fly it, then I should be—"

Smoke, his eyes a little glassy, stared at the trim low-wing pursuit job on which rested all his hopes. "But I haven't any other, Mel. Not one."

"You told me three days ago that you had ordered the engine, and that the parts for another were being cast for assembly. And if you think I'm going to allow you to enter Girard's—" She stopped, realizing that she had released the cat.

"So you want to keep me away from Girard!" said Smoke, slowly.

"Oh, Smoke, there's no use avoiding the issue. He's saying around the clubs that you're going to be sorry you tried to buck him. Father told me last night, and father should know."

"That was a pretty crude attempt, Mel."

She stood up, and he also rose, looking down at her uptilted face.

"I'm taking the man-killer away from you, Smoke Burnham. And I'm taking it because I think too much of you to let anything harm you. I don't care what methods I use. No woman ever cares, where her man is involved. But if you want to make it difficult—don't let's quarrel, Smoke. Please don't. You have plenty of money. You can give all this up."

He started to walk away and then stopped, turning slowly. His hair sparkled in the sun, but there was no sparkle to his eyes. They were dead.

"All right, Mel," he said. "The plane is yours. I told you that it was, and you have the title to prove it. I'll . . . I'll send it over to your field." He walked away from her toward the hangar.

She watched him for a moment before she went toward the car. A dampness was clinging to her eyelashes. Hurriedly she made her way to the roadster, got in, and sent the car screaming back to town.

In the shadow of the hangar, Smoke told Alex what had happened.

Alex would not believe it. "You can't let her do that, Smoke! It's bad enough to be broke when you have a chance of recouping the works. Listen. Tell the girl that you're flat, Smoke."

Smoke shrugged.

"I can't, Alex. I'm . . . I'm afraid she'd leave me. All her crowd has money. Plenty of it."

"But she'll make you give up—"

Smoke squared his shoulders and smiled. "I read something in the *SP* a few days ago. By a fellow named Yochin. It goes:

> "Flight! It is a thrilling thing,
> Beloved by all us guys,
> But if your pash is for the Wing,
> Boy, oh boy, be wise!
>
> "Never take yourself a frau,
> Though she be sweet and shy;
> For she will say, 'I've got you now,
> And you must never fly.
>
> "'There's danger in that flying tub.
> I'll teach you bridge, my dear;
> So keep away from the Pilot's Club.
> No hangar tales! No beer!'"

CHAPTER THREE

Girard's International

THE airport was beaten by the prop wash of a dozen ships until it was little more than a square chunk of dust-fog lined with gray-coated spectators. Men rushed importantly to and fro, carrying papers, soft drinks and microphone wires, bearing bright-colored ribbons which were labeled "Official."

Other men, attired in flannel slacks, suspenders and felt hats, stood by and eyed each other speculatively. These men were pilots, utterly indistinguishable from the rest so far as clothing went. Boots, shiny helmets and suede jackets were for the men who had to dress the part to be recognized as one of the flying fraternity.

In a special stand constructed of new boards sat a group of men who were dominated by the central figure—Girard. Girard was watching all things as though he owned them, and before his eyes danced the columns of figures which meant circulation, and therefore advertising, and therefore money in the bank.

Girard turned to a secretary who was as plain as his name—Smith. "There's that Burnham now. Tell him to come over here." Sitting back and holding his cane as one holds a scepter, Girard smiled easily. His blue jowl wobbled.

Smoke Burnham, his yellow hair undimmed by the dust,

stood twisting a pair of gigantic goggles round and round by their strap, listening to Alex Montague.

Montague faced a pilot known as Lefty, and Lefty's eyes were wobbly. "See here, now, Lefty, old fellow. You haven't any use for that old ZT in the hangar. We just want to borrow it for an hour or so. Smoke doesn't want to fly the Mystery Plane before all these people, Lefty." Alex rested his hand on Lefty's shoulder and regarded him man to man. "Remember the time we were all down at Baton Rouge, Lefty? For old times' sake—"

Smith arrived as Lefty said, "But, Alex, I've got a sale for that ZT. Besides, it's a man-killer among man-killers. The flying wires are almost rusted through. I wouldn't let Smoke fly it."

"What about the buyer?"

"The buyer? Oh, that's different. He—well, what the guy doesn't know won't hurt him. But if you cracked up the crate, Smoke, I'd never forgive myself."

"We'll guarantee the price," said Alex, heartily. One hand in his pocket was playing with three pennies he had won in an hour's matching on one borrowed cent. This was the entire capital of Burnham Aeronautical Company.

Smith coughed three times before they knew that he was there. "Pardon the intrusion, gentlemen, but Girard—"

"To hell with Girard," said Alex, turning back to Lefty.

Smith was more persistent than a man without a chin is expected to be. Perhaps that was because Girard's eyes were hot on his back.

"Girard says," said Smith, "that you can have the new racer—the red one—that he bought from Baird Aeronautics."

Smoke blinked. "You mean Girard is giving me a ship?"

"Why, certainly!" replied Smith. "That is, he's lending you one. This is the qualification race for the International Air Derby, you must remember, Burnham. He wants you to qualify from this district."

"Is that why he withdrew one of his own pilots and sent him to the next district?" said Smoke.

"What do you mean, International Air Derby?" barked Alex.

"Just that," said Smith. "International. All the publicity is being released on it today, and in six weeks the race will start. We . . . we didn't want to raise too much dust until we had something like this qualification try to back it up. Now with three men qualified from each district, we can state that the race is an actuality. It's very good publicity, Montague."

"But why International?" Alex persisted.

Smith coughed. "Everyone will know just before the race starts. This is something that has never been attempted before. And unless you qualify, you can't fly in the derby."

To himself, Smoke mentioned the fact that if he didn't win the derby, he'd have to take the Mystery Ship away from Mel and present it to Girard, so that Girard could claim all the credit for developing it. To himself, Smoke said, "Damn!"

To Smith, Smoke said, "Why is he so keen on having me enter?"

"Why," replied Smith, "for the publicity that goes with your name. If you don't enter—" He realized then that cats were escaping their confines and clamped his chinless mouth quite shut.

"You'd think the guy wanted me to win!" frowned Smoke.

Alex also frowned. He was thinking that three pennies didn't even buy a cup of coffee. "What's the final prize money?"

"Fifty thousand dollars," Smith said promptly. "That's for first prize. You chaps are all in the money if you win. It would cost Girard a half million to build that factory for—" He blinked and swallowed, his watery eyes taking in the people around them to make certain that he had not been overheard.

"Do you want the red racer?" demanded Smith, remembering his errand.

Smoke gave the goggles an extra twist and shook his yellow hair so violently that it cascaded down into his eyes. *"No!"*

As though driven back by the force of the word, Smith half ran to the stand where Girard sat. When he had reached there, Girard was seen to turn a faint purple, although he did not stop nodding to the people who were passing by.

"What did you say 'No!' for?" cried Alex, waving dramatic hands. "He wants us in, we'll go in. We could qualify in that red crate! What the hell—?"

Smoke's deep blue eyes were as quiet as a summer sky. He gave the goggles another twist and shrugged. "Ever play chess, Alex?"

"Certainly. But it takes brains to play chess."

"And it takes brains to get and keep circulation." Smoke looked over at Girard. "That guy is playing chess, and no mistake, Alex. This is all good, clean sport, this racing. Nothing up my sleeves, no mad hatters in my hat. In chess you never take the man that is offered for you to take. That's what the enemy wants. If you take his offered piece, he can immediately walk in with the plan he has in mind.

"No, Alex, that red knight is going to stay on the board, untouched. We'll use the ZT, flying wires or no."

Lefty shook his head. "Cripes, you guys are persistent! But if you don't care any more for Smoke's neck than that, Alex, the green crate is all yours. What was that about a two-thousand guarantee in case you crack it up?"

"Lefty," said Alex with great solemnity, "you've got some shylock in your blood after all. We guarantee the two thousand in case of a crash." He rubbed the three pennies together and tried to pretend they were at least dimes.

"Sure," said Lefty. "I know you guys are okay for the two grand. Smoke Burnham's name on a piece of paper is good enough for me."

Without turning a single yellow hair, Smoke reached for his pilot's log and scribbled and signed a contract to that effect. He and Alex immediately made their way through the crowd to the hangars wherein reposed the sickly green ZT, once monarch of the speedways, but now just a second-rate man-killer.

ZTs were never so much as ships went, though they went fast enough. Their tails were short and stubby—which looked all right, but worked wrong. The airstream from the gigantic cowl sometimes forgot to touch the flippers and rudder, and therefore a ZT in a power dive was the same as a silver-handled casket without the silver handles.

Racing ships have come far since those days and you'll

find that most present racing ships carry out the ZT's major points. But just the same, it doesn't detract from their status—man-killer!

When the ZT was warming on the line, Smoke stood mournfully by, looking at the single cockpit. Melanie King, resplendent in a sport suit straight from London, came up, her eyes fastened on the ramshackle crate.

"Smoke!" she cried. "You're . . . you're not going to fly that?"

"Sure," said Smoke. "It's got a stick and motor and everything. The only thing about it is that I've got to leave Patty because there's only one office. And that's bad luck."

"You wouldn't have to worry about luck," said Mel slowly, "if you had any regard for—for your own neck."

"My own neck?" replied Smoke. "Why, what's the matter with this ship?"

"Oh, Smoke, please don't act that way! All you worry about is speed, speed, speed! And more speed. 'How fast will they go? How far can I lash them on? I can fly it faster than that!'"

Gently and reproachfully, thinking about the trim Mystery Ship in King's hangar, Alex laid his hand on her shoulder. "If you hadn't taken away his toys, Mel—"

"So that's it!" She drew her slight height very straight and thrust indignant hands into her pockets. "You're trying to work on my sympathy with this ZT. You're crude, both of you. Fly it for all I care, Smoke Burnham!"

She whirled and in an instant she was swallowed in the crowd and dry, eddying dust.

"Ain't she a little hellcat?" said Smoke, admiringly. He looked up at Alex with a pleased grin.

In spite of the three cents, the ZT, the chess-playing of Girard, Alex could not help laughing. He understood things, did Alex.

That inevitable, unvarying patter of puns and general good-fellowship was drooling out of the microphone over the hangar.

"And now, ladies and gentlemen, we are all set for the qualifying race for the great International Air Derby. You, ladies and gentlemen, are privileged for the first time to hear the details of this great contest which is being sponsored by Paul Harrison Girard.

"The International Air Derby, ladies and gentlemen, will include ships of all nations, ships of all types. It will be the supreme contest of man's conquest of the air.

"The planes that place and qualify today in all the several districts will be allowed to try for this fifty-thousand-dollar prize.

"The race will start in a few weeks from Washington, DC. The dauntless pilots will wing their intrepid way from that city to Miami. From there to Panama, over the treacherous Caribbean. From Panama to Chile. From Chile across the suicidal Andes, and across the unplumbed jungles to Rio de Janeiro. Back to Panama, and from there to California. There will ensue a mad dash from California back to Washington, DC.

"Paul Harrison Girard has offered a prize of fifty thousand dollars to the winner.

"And now today we have on this field such famous, intrepid birdmen as Smoke Burnham, speed king of the skyways—"

Alex smiled in satisfaction.

Smoke said, "If the police found out you'd killed an announcer, what would they do?"

"I wasn't aware the police gave medals," replied Alex. "Say, is that engine sputtering on all nine or what?"

"Or what," said Smoke. "But if it doesn't stop or-whatting very soon, we'll have to steal the Mystery Ship, give it to Girard, and go get us a couple of shovels to dig ditches."

Mel was coming up to them and her eyes were on Smoke. She swallowed hard before she started to speak.

"Smoke. A man was just telling me what happened one time to a man who flew one of these ZTs. This man said that the ship suddenly flipped over in the air, darted for the ground and burst into flames. They . . . they never found the pilot."

Smoke smiled and touched her shoulder for an instant. Then he found a helmet, pulled it down and adjusted the goggles. He threw a leg over the pit and slid down, immediately gunning the few hundred horses which bellowed and strained under the cowl.

Speech was impossible. Dust whipped and stung. The ZT began to roll for the starting line.

Mel buried her face in Alex's rough tweed coat. "Don't . . . don't let him kill himself, Alex. Please don't let him! I . . . I love him, Alex."

Alex fingered the three pennies and wondered if it was worth the price. . . .

*Mel buried her face in Alex's rough tweed coat.
"Don't . . . don't let him kill himself, Alex.
Please don't let him! I . . . I love him, Alex."*

CHAPTER FOUR

Fifty Thousand if—!

THE ZT shivered—not from anticipation, but from motor vibration. The wires made long, blurred slashes leading down to the wings. The small spatted wheels rolled over the uneven ground. Taxiing the ship was a man's job, and Smoke Burnham was weary when he reached the starting line.

Far down the field a mechanic was swinging the flag—the warning flag. In a moment he would pick up his green banner, and green means takeoff.

The ships would leave the line at ten-second intervals and charge down straight at that mechanic, everything in the fire. But before they reached him, the wings would be lightening, the wheels would be off, and pilots would be chewing up altitude in a scramble to make every horsepower count. Before each pilot's eyes hovered a vision of stacked bills. Fifty thousand dollars if they qualified and *if* they won the International Air Derby.

But a pilot is an optimistic soul. He has to be. He's a smooth-nerved, clear-eyed bit of human machinery. There is no room for the blond-haired lad who stands up on the silver screen, throws back his chair with chattering teeth and screams out that he can't stand it, he can't stand it! He dreams he is falling in flames and that his wings are gone!

If a pilot thinks that at all, he never lets on, even to himself.

He can't. Nothing heroic about it. If he doesn't toe the mark on that, he is no longer a pilot. He goes and keeps books for some paunched business mogul.

The ZT, the classic man-killer, might shake in every rib, might knock in every cylinder, but Smoke Burnham's right hand was steady on the stick and his left hand was lightly stroking the throttle as he looked about him.

Caldwell, confessed black sheep of the sky tracks, was crouching at Smoke's right. Smoke waved and Caldwell waved back. However, that wouldn't keep Caldwell from spilling Smoke if Smoke asked for it.

Raymond, sometimes making news for Girard, was close by Smoke's left, in a brilliant orange ship that was mostly engine. Raymond pretended that he did not see Smoke's greeting.

Smoke shrugged and smiled simultaneously. So Raymond wasn't waving today! Maybe he was afraid the ZT would collapse in the air and scatter pieces into the prop of that orange charger.

Thinking about this, Smoke fastened the straps of his chute around his legs, across his chest. It was a silk exhibition chute, twenty-eight feet in diameter, and it let a man land at nine miles per hour. Alex had borrowed it from somewhere.

Smoke, watching the mechanic select the green flag, remembered that a cup of coffee, hours before, had been his sole diet that day. Maybe, even if he didn't win, he could have Alex coax the winner to throw a party. Smoke wondered what all these people, all these pilots, would think if they knew Smoke Burnham was broke.

'Twas ever thus!

The mechanic whipped the flag and the first ship yowled out of the line like a projectile and charged the white circle.

Feet on brakes, Smoke opened up his motor and waited, counting. "Five, six, seven, eight, nine—"

The second ship slammed down the runway after the first. Smoke wished Patty could have been there. Bad luck to fly without Patty. She hadn't liked being shut up in his room. He'd probably—

The third plane bellowed a war cry and lashed air in a two-hundred-mile-an-hour climb toward the sky.

She'd probably have all the curtains ripped up and the stuffing out of the chairs when he got back. Wouldn't do . . .

The fourth plane, Caldwell, jumped out of position and careened across the earth, almost immediately flashing cloudward.

Wouldn't do to let the hotel manager know. Bad enough not to pay his bill. "Five, six, seven, eight, nine—"

The ZT's brakes were off. The tail jumped into flying position, blasted up by the slipstream alone. The ground was a khaki blur under the pounding wheels. The motor shattered the skies with its *haroom . . . haroom . . . haroom. . . .*

At fifty feet, Smoke leveled out and streaked after Caldwell.

Everything was a great panorama of unidentified color. Green trees, tan fields, white faces, red planes, all merged into a rushing composite which meant one thing—*speed*!

The man-killers were all in the sky.

Six engines hammered strident sounds into one mighty ear-shattering discord. Six sets of wings flashed between clouds and clods. Six pilots hunched forward as though that would help, and visualized stacks of green money.

Or did they visualize the money? Were they thinking about a few letters on a white sheet of paper? Publicity?

Or was it speed?

Four and a half times faster than a smoothbore cannonball had ever traveled, six men flashed down the sky.

A checkered red-and-white pyramid came up between the two top cylinders of the ZT's motor. The pyramid was vertical and then suddenly horizontal. Smoke was glued to the chute. Blood left his head, drawn by the centrifugal force. Everything was black for the smallest fraction of a minute.

Another pylon was far ahead, vertical.

Raymond gained ten feet of altitude, leveled off, gained another ten, leveled off. Looking back, Smoke could see goggles flashing through the silvery disc of a slashing prop. When he looked again he could see only the wheels of the orange monoplane. The wheels were growing larger. The striping was distinct.

Raymond was diving in over Smoke's head.

Smoke's first impulse was to dive out from under. Instead, he poured on another notch of throttle and nosed slightly up.

Over the side of the orange plane Smoke saw Raymond's goggles. The orange ship zoomed to avoid the ZT's upthrust nose. Raymond was behind again.

Khaki ground sliding so close below that Smoke thought he could reach over and pick up a rock. Perhaps, if this came out, the khaki ground would give place to fetid green of jungles. And the green of jungles to the insurmountable Andes—snow-covered peaks, bare rock . . .

The ZT was creeping up on Caldwell. The man-killer of past days was proving that it still could do a thing or two.

Why, Smoke wondered, had they thought a speed race would qualify anyone for the jungles and mountains? Then it would be navigation, blind flight, poor gas, tortured, oxygen-starved engines. And Girard, the worst hurdle of all . . .

Caldwell was finding a split instant to look back. Caldwell's lean, brown face was ghoulish behind his goggles. The yellow plane which Caldwell flew yawed a few feet. Just a warning not to cut through.

A heat bump from the center of a field came up and rapped the underside of the ZT. Smoke fought the stick for an instant. The area of rapidly rising air was longer than it should have been. The ZT went up twenty feet, still remaining horizontal.

Smoke dived. Caldwell's upturned face flickered briefly. Smoke shot down over the yellow plane's prop. The yellow nose was coming up like a javelin. Smoke went on down. Caldwell, razzing his engine, tried to drive Smoke back.

Yellow prop less than five feet from green fuselage, Smoke held on. One of them had to break.

Caldwell's face was tight in the face of an imminent crash. His hand on the stick was white, his eyes were murderous.

His left hand came back on the throttle. The yellow ship dived away and the green ship hurtled on through.

Smoke grinned into the slipstream. The black sheep had lost his nerve. Smoke did not stop to think that Smoke

Burnham would have lost his life and that Caldwell had saved two necks. You don't think of those things at four and a half times the speed of a cannonball.

Looking back, Smoke saw that Raymond was also over Caldwell. Raymond was pulling on through.

A red-and-white pylon went horizontal, came back vertical. Smoke charged for the last pylon. The ZT shivered under the strain of too much speed.

Smoke was thinking about the maddening part of air races. You never know whether or not you've won until the judges get out their slide rules and pencils and figure the seconds, the fifths of seconds—as though anyone can see a fifth of a second, when it takes more than half a second to bat an eye.

The crowd was rushing up toward him as he dived in toward the finish line. He had a hasty impression of open mouths, flailing arms.

Raymond was behind the ZT. And behind Raymond something flashed against the turquoise sky. Caldwell was coming in to capture the lead!

A yellow spear went across Raymond's prop disc. A yellow cowl was above the ZT's tail.

Raymond's orange ship stayed where it was, boring straight at the yellow plane's belly. Caldwell had broken once. Would he break again?

But Caldwell saw too late. The yellow ship slipped sideways. The three other planes in the race were almost abreast. The air was a kaleidoscope of props and colored wings. Abruptly they were scrambled.

Raymond had not counted upon Caldwell's ignoring him. He held his place just an instant too long. Then it was up to Caldwell.

Smoke's eyes were all for the finishing line. The first thing he noticed was a jar which ran through the entire ship.

Caldwell's wheels were in the ZT's tail surfaces!

Both man-killers hurtled upward, out of the way of other men.

Caldwell tried to fight free. Spruce, steel tubing and linen exploded together!

Battered by fragments, drowned in noise, Smoke tried to scramble out of the pit. He was upside down, with wings and shattered props between himself and the sky. He saw Caldwell trying to get out.

The judge's stand was below, seen by looking up. At four times the speed of a cannonball, the maimed ships smashed straight ahead through the sky, over the finish line.

Smoke shook away from the pit. His fingers were already pulling his rip cord. He didn't know where the ground might be. He expected the chute to foul and carry him on in with the wreckage. But he pulled the ring.

Hammers were slammed into his ribs. He swung crazily from horizontal, through vertical and back up again. As he slapped down, the ground was under him.

He threw off his goggles, drew up his legs. Khaki earth smashed into his back.

For a half-minute an hour long he tried to breathe, tried to get air into his collapsed chest. But he wasn't thinking about air.

Smoke shook away from the pit. His fingers were already pulling his rip cord. He didn't know where the ground might be.

His agony-dimmed eyes registered nothing of the field about him. Towed by the chute across the rough runway, Smoke was remembering that Melanie King's eyes were never the same. Sometimes blue, sometimes darker, almost ebony. Sometimes tender, sometimes mocking. There was something vital about knowing it.

Hands were on him, lifting him to his feet. When he could focus his glance, he saw that he had landed within thirty feet of the stand.

The crackle of fire was in the air and he whirled about. White heat was coming from tangled rubbish in the center of the field.

Smoke tried to talk. "Caldwell! Did he—?"

They held him up. Someone said, "He didn't make it. His chute tangled in the fins and he rode her in. There isn't any use—"

Mel was there, and Alex was keeping her back. Smoke looked at her and grinned a sick grin. Then he looked down at his hands. A thick oozing trickle of blood was dripping from his palm, running down his fingers, down to the khaki earth. The wound felt hot and wet and deep.

Girard was there, standing with his hands on his hips, smiling at Smoke, his unfinished face flabby and loose.

"Well, it happens to everybody," Girard said. "You're lucky to get out of it. I told that fellow Raymond not to cut you too close. There's publicity coming aplenty, Burnham. You'll be worth a mint of circulation in this race. I wanted you in. That's why I told Raymond—"

Smoke looked up with his pain-racked eyes boring into Girard's unfinished face.

"Publicity? Circulation? What does Caldwell know about a headline—now?" Smoke's tone was weary, monotonous. He was merely asking a question that he wanted answered. Desperately he wanted it answered.

"Why should you worry, Burnham?" said Girard. "You're in. If Caldwell had—"

Suddenly Smoke's open palm lashed out and cracked against Girard's jowl. The hand fell back, limp. Smoke's knees caved gradually, gradually. Alex helped carry him to the ambulance.

A streak of thick, black-red blood was on Girard's jowl. Hot, salty blood, startling against the pallor of his face—like a brand. . . .

CHAPTER FIVE

Girard Takes a Trick

ACROSS the gray sky from which the sun had gone floated an airliner, its wings defined by red and green sparks—running lights. The soft whir of the engines lingered in the twilight until the gentle crunch of wheels against earth ended the flight.

The remaining rays of the sun outlined spindly clouds, tingeing them with a faint red.

Mel King sighed and rose from the folding chair outside the Pilot's Club. Smoke started to get up, but she pressed him back with a touch of her slender hand.

"Don't, Smoke. You aren't well enough."

Smoke snorted, and grinned. "All right, Mel. If you'd had your way about it, I would have been in bed a year instead of a month."

"Before I go, Smoky, tell me once and for all. Are you really entering that Air Derby to South America?"

Smoke sighed and watched the darkening sky.

"But you have no ship, Smoke. None at all. And I won't release the rights or title of the Mystery Plane."

"I'm not asking you to," he said gently.

"But you want me to. Smoky, I'd do anything for you. You know that. But I don't . . . don't want to lose you, that's all. When I think of the jungles and the Andes, I—"

"Too late to think of that," said Smoke. "I've committed myself. The papers—"

"Oh, the papers! Print on a white page! You're not a publicity hound, Smoke. Not a bit of it."

Alex Montague rounded the edge of the building and came on, his dark, excitable eyes gleaming like a car's headlights—or almost as brightly. At the sight of Mel he stopped and removed his hat with a bow.

She nodded to him and walked toward the roadster. Slamming the door, she started the purring motor. Her brace of red lights was gone, melting with the swarm on the highway.

"Another fight?" asked Alex.

"No," said Smoke. "Just a one-sided argument. What's the news, Alex? You're all apuff."

"Listen, Smoke. See here!" He thrust a paper under Smoke's nose. It was a short space, small print, no head. In the fading light Smoke could hardly read it.

"Sure," said Smoke. "It says the Hedstrom plant has just turned out an airliner that can go three hundred or better. What of it?"

"We'll make a stab at getting one!"

Smoke grinned and fished for a cigarette. Finding none, he relaxed and continued to grin. "Those things only cost about fifty thousand, Alex. What is the state of finance?"

Alex paced restlessly back and forth. "Don't joke about it, Smoke. We've got to do something. Here it is within two days of the race and we've got no plane. That's a hell of a shape to be in! We'll have—"

"—To steal a Hedstrom to get one," finished Smoke. "Now

let me see. There's a note for two thousand on the ZT. And a hospital bill for eight hundred on me. And a hotel bill of four hundred for both of us. And my watch brought three dollars yesterday."

"Smoke," said Alex, placing his hand on Smoke's shoulder, man to man, "why don't you listen to reason? It's all for your own good, old fellow. We need a plane and we need funds. We've *got* to have backing. If we don't, we'll be on the rocks, sued right and left. It's only because people think you've got money that they keep off us for these bills. And that won't go on long. If we don't do something about it soon, we'll have to steal that Mystery Ship from Mel and give it to Girard. And he'll get the credit for three years of your work."

Smoke was grinning, teeth flashing in the darkness. "Be human, Alex, and forget the high-pressure salesmanship. What do you intend to do?"

"It's you, Smoke. Now listen. Old Man King has plenty of money—many, many millions more than he needs. And as a special favor to his future son-in-law, he'd think nothing of lending you—"

"Alex, how many times have I got to turn that down? This is the second time today. You're wearing me out with that line. I'm *not* going to ask King for money just because of Mel. That's out!"

"All right, all right," said Alex, backing off. "I know what you're afraid of. You think if Mel King finds out you're broke, she'll give you the gate. You're afraid to put it to a test. You're *yellow*, Smoke!"

Smoke stared through the dusk, listening to the faraway

drone of a mail plane traveling north. Mel would also hear it and look up at it.

Smoke's voice was almost inaudible. "Yes, Alex, I'm yellow."

"Hell, Smoke! I'm sorry. But everything is—well, sort of up in the air, and I'm worried about you. It'll break your heart if you have to turn that ship over to Girard. And I know—"

"Forget it, Alex. I know what you mean. Women and wings—I guess they don't mix so well."

"Oh, come on, now, Smoke. Don't go moody on me. We've got a tough enough nut to crack without that. What are we going to do?"

"Steal the Mystery Plane and use it. It's a two-cockpit job and it will qualify."

Alex shook his head. "Don't joke about it, Smoke. You go from one extreme to the other."

"I mean it." Smoke got up and looked toward the operations office, which was glittering with lights. A man came out and approached the Pilot's Club. He stopped and touched Smoke's arm.

"How's it going?" he said.

"Okay, Ben. Listen, Ben. Are you taking the Nine out?"

Ben smiled at Smoke. "Want to use my car? Go ahead."

Smoke stepped off in the direction of the parking line. Alex, shaking his head doubtfully, followed.

Humming something about a dying aviator, Smoke cheerfully climbed in and started the engine. Alex slammed the door.

"You're not kidding me, Smoke?"

"No. We're going to steal the ship out of the King hangar,

repaint it tonight, and use it in the race." He was about to pull out when Patty thrust her feline nose up at the window, pleading. She had been asleep and her gaze was reproachful when she discovered she had not been invited.

Smoke climbed out and opened the rumble seat. The hunting leopard did not seem to exert an ounce of strength. She flowed into the seat and curled up, content at the sound of the engine.

The hangar at the King estate was lighted, its open doors loosing a yellow glare which lay upon the concrete runway, a splotch of life in dead darkness.

Smoke Burnham eased the car into a lane that flanked the field, cutting off the engine. He stepped out and looked toward the squat building. Alex stepped down beside him and stared over his shoulder.

"Why should the hangar be lighted at this time of night?" demanded Alex.

"Maybe Mel's tucking the Mystery Plane in bed. Come on."

"You're not going right down there, are you?"

"Why not? If no one's there, I'll fly the plane out. And if someone is there, I'll make my apologies. But I refuse to be a sneak thief, Alex."

Wearily, Alex plodded behind him toward the hangar. Patty hopped down from the rumble seat, a shadow of rippling muscles, and stalked third in the procession. A man who did not know Patty would have been startled out of his wits. A cheetah is not a heartening companion in the dark—it looks too much like a leopard and its teeth and claws are much too long.

A sound of voices came from the interior, softened by distance and darkness. They were immediately followed by the roar of an engine—the engine of the Mystery Ship, unmistakable to Smoke.

Smoke broke into a loping run. The engine rose in crescendo. A hand on the throttle was gunning nervously.

Rounding the edge of the doors, Smoke came to a halt. He stared up at the mighty disc of a whirling prop. It was advancing toward him!

"Stop!" he bellowed, but his voice was unheard in the din of engine and racketing club. The plane was gathering speed, bound for the field.

Smoke sprang to one side, trying to grab at a wing. The low foil was elusive and he tripped and fell to the concrete.

A white face was visible for an instant over the cockpit rim, and then the Mystery Plane hurtled down the runway and into the blackness.

Jumping up, Smoke scrutinized the hangar interior. A door slammed at the far end. Smoke leaped toward the sound. A dun-colored streak went by—Patty.

Outside the hangar a scream shrilled. It was immediately followed by a tinkle of glass. When Smoke reached the rear door, it was ajar.

Patty's snarling cry was hair-raising. Smoke laid hands on a twisting body which strove mightily to get away. Patty stood back, licking her lips, thoroughly enjoying herself, waiting to get into the fray once more. Trained to give chase to anything which would run, Patty thought that the quarry was hers, and hers alone.

The man Smoke held was suddenly aware that hands were upon him. Redoubling his efforts, the quarry slid to one side. In the darkness, footing was precarious. Smoke suddenly found himself holding an empty coat.

Patty was off again. Gears clashed, and Patty howled as though in pain. Headlights streaked across the field and a car hurtled away.

Patty came back disconsolately, limping, but she bore a patch of ragged cloth in her sharp teeth.

Smoke swore loudly and at some length. He slammed the coat down to the ground.

Alex materialized like a genie. "Who was it?"

Smoke stopped swearing. "He forgot to give me his card," he said sarcastically. Then he looked down at the coat and towed it into the hangar lights. He delved in its breast pocket and brought forth a wallet.

The name, stamped in gold on leather, was "J.C. Smith." When Smoke opened it, a sheaf of greenbacks came to light. He pulled out the bills and counted them.

"Five hundred dollars," he said.

"Smith," said Alex. "Girard's secretary!"

"Sure it is. Girard wants this plane and he wants it bad. Well, he got it."

"But we can press suit," said Alex.

"Certainly we can. And he'd claim it was all a mistake or something. We haven't a leg to support us, Alex. He controls the headlines. We won't even be able to prove that Girard took it. And if we pressed suit too hard, then we'd wake up and find ourselves very accomplished daisy-pushers."

"But, damn it, why should he steal the thing?"

"He needs it, that's why. After all those promises to give the government the best pursuit ship ever built, he'd look silly not being able to hand it over. Then there's prestige connected with it. And circulation—and therefore, much, much money. He's got us, Alex, and there's no use hollering about it."

"But aren't you going to make a fight?"

"Sure. In the International Air Derby."

"Wait," said Alex pensively. "There's something about this—something— Look here, Smoke. He couldn't have been so wary of our winning this race. We haven't even got a ship, and he knows it. Listen, Smoke. This is serious. He . . . he knows if we take that International Air Derby, we'll—"

"We'll what?" Smoke demanded.

"He knows we'll never come back," Alex finished quietly. "He's set a trap for us if we ever take off. If we got lost down there, we wouldn't be able to turn the Mystery Ship over to him."

Alex sighed. "Yes, and I just happened to think that Smoke Burnham lost would bring plenty of publicity and money for Girard. He could play it up for weeks and weeks. Searching planes, searching parties on the ground. Threshing through the wilds and jungles of Brazil. And, of course, they'd never find us."

Smoke shook his head, bleakly. "Well, I don't feel so bad about that five hundred bucks."

"Neither do I. We'll charge them that for plane rental while we're gone. And boy, could I eat a big, juicy steak with—"

Another voice cut in and Patty sat up straight, expecting more excitement. It was Mel King.

She came into the hangar with quick, rapid steps. Her eyes were hot coals and her shoulders were as straight as a toy soldier's.

"Smoke," she said, coming to a stop. "Where is that plane?"

"Plane! Why, they took it, of course. How are you, Mel?"

She stepped close to him. "You're lying, Smoke Burnham. You stole that ship. What are you, an Indian giver? A sneak thief? Because I took it away from you so that you'd live long enough to—" She turned and walked away, back toward the mansion on the hill. Her shoulders were no longer straight, her splendid head no longer erect.

Smoke would have followed her, but Alex stopped him. "You can't convince her, Smoke. She's a woman, worrying about her man. Don't blame her. She'll come around all right. Let's leave here and get something to eat."

Smoke turned slowly around. He was smiling with set lips. "I'll say she's going to come around," he muttered.

"Meaning what?"

"Wait and see, Alex, wait and see. We're grabbing the first train out for the Hedstrom plant. That new transport plane is going to win the International Air Derby, Girard or no Girard. And in spite of Melanie King. Let's go."

Patty cat-footed in their wake, still clinging to the scrap of cloth.

CHAPTER SIX

Smoke Gets His Chance

THE president of the Hedstrom plant was very affable, extremely courteous. When he had waved Smoke and Alex to chairs and passed the cigars and cigarettes, he leaned back, placed his thumbs in his broad vest, and said, "Now, gentlemen, what can I do for you? It isn't every day that we get a chance to serve Smoke Burnham."

"We," said Smoke, as evenly as possible, "want to fly your new Super-Comet airliner in the International Air Derby."

Hedstrom blinked and swung forward. "Why, I'm very sorry, gentlemen, but you see we have only the one experimental ship and all the bugs haven't been ironed out in it."

Smoke looked at Alex, and Alex stood up, waving airy hands. "Mr. Hedstrom, I'm surprised that you do not think any more of Burnham's ability than that! What, may I ask, are a few bugs to Smoke Burnham? And how, may I ask, do you intend to get this plane before the public eye? You had a small, unheaded line in yesterday's paper about your speed record for transports. That right?"

"Yes," said Hedstrom. "You see, Mr. Montague, we haven't been releasing very heavy because we don't think we're quite ready to—"

Alex leaned dramatically forward. "Hedstrom, do you want

this new liner on every airline in the country? Do you want Super-Comet to be synonymous with reliability and speed? Do you want headlines? Headlines, man! Screaming banners all carrying the name Super-Comet! It would be on every man's tongue. You'd hear it in the barbershops, in the hotels. Everyone would be standing back gaping in amazement when the name was mentioned.

"The name Hedstrom would go thundering down the hall of time as the greatest in all aviation! You would be able to build plants a hundred times the size of this. And yet, Hedstrom, you sit there and tell me that you are doubtful. Doubtful of what? Are you casting reflection upon your engineers? Upon your ships? Upon your own product? No, Hedstrom, certainly not *that*!"

Hedstrom swallowed hard. In spite of himself, his eyes were as round and big as dollars, sparkling with their vision of the future as painted by that master painter Alex Montague. He came to himself with a jolt, and something of shrewdness replaced his excitement.

"You're anxious to get this plane, aren't you?" he said.

"Oh," shrugged Alex, "perhaps, and perhaps not. The planes to be had are too numerous to mention. But, like all the rest of my softhearted breed, I looked at that sick little unheaded scrap of nothing in the paper and said to myself, 'Alex, that man needs publicity. He has something there. And if he isn't backed up, aviation is doomed to lose one of the greatest developments of the day.'"

The gleam was still there. Small drops of sweat were on Alex's brow.

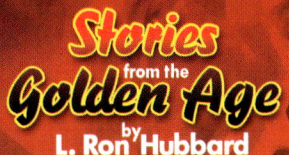

Join the Stories from the Golden Age Book Club Today!

Yes! Sign me up for the Book Club (*check one of the following*) and each month I will receive:
○ One paperback book at $9.95 a month.
○ Or, one unabridged audiobook CD at the cost of $9.95 a month.

Book Club members get FREE SHIPPING and handling (applies to US residents only).

_____
Name   (please print)

_____
If under 18, signature of guardian

_____
Address

_____
City   State   ZIP   Telephone

_____
E-mail

You may sign up by doing any of the following:
1. To pay by credit card go online at www.goldenagestories.com
2. Call toll-free 1-877-842-5299 or fax this card in to 1-323-466-7817
3. Send in this card with a check for the first month payable to Galaxy Press

To get a FREE Stories from the Golden Age catalog check here ○ and mail or fax in this card.

Thank you!

And get a FREE gift.

For details, go to www.goldenagestories.com.

For an up-to-date listing of available titles visit www.goldenagestories.com
YOU CAN CANCEL AT ANY TIME AND RETURN THE BOOK AND AUDIO FOR A FULL REFUND.
Prices are set in US dollars only. For non-US residents, please call 1-323-466-7815 for pricing information or go to www.goldenagestories.com. Terms, prices and conditions are subject to change. Subscription is subject to acceptance.

© 2008 Galaxy Press, LLC. All Rights Reserved.

NO POSTAGE
NECESSARY
IF MAILED
IN THE
UNITED STATES

BUSINESS REPLY MAIL
FIRST-CLASS MAIL   PERMIT NO. 75738   LOS ANGELES CA

POSTAGE WILL BE PAID BY ADDRESSEE

GOLDEN AGE BOOK CLUB
GALAXY PRESS
7051 HOLLYWOOD BLVD
LOS ANGELES CA 90028-9771

"Montague," said Hedstrom, "you seem very confident of winning this race."

"No chance of losing in any plane with Smoke Burnham at the controls," said Alex.

"Then I'll make you a proposition, Montague. You can buy the Super-Comet from me, and if you win, I'll refund the price."

Alex stared at Smoke. They couldn't have purchased an aileron of the big ship if the whole thing sold for a thousand dollars.

"How much do you want?" said Alex.

Hedstrom shrugged.

"You can have her cheap, Montague, because, after all, Smoke Burnham is Smoke Burnham. Fifty thousand dollars is the price."

Alex spread out his hands. "Cheap, Hedstrom. Cheap enough. Here, Smoke, sign a note for fifty thousand and give it to the man."

Smoke reached for paper and pen, but Hedstrom said, "A note?"

"Certainly a note," cried Alex. "You wouldn't for a moment try to tell me that Smoke Burnham's credit is no good."

"Oh, certainly not, Montague, but—"

"But what?" demanded Alex. "Sign the note, Smoke. We haven't any time to get this ship ready as it is."

"But I—" began Hedstrom.

Alex picked up the telephone, pulled up the receiver and handed it to Hedstrom. "Call your plant and tell them to run the Super-Comet out on the runway."

There is something not to be denied about the way central says "Number please? Number please?" Hedstrom gave her the number, and Smoke completed and signed the contract.

"There," said Smoke. "Now for your signature, Hedstrom."

Having completed his call, Hedstrom blinked twice, saw that Alex was about to start talking again, and signed.

Two days later a mammoth sea-sky bird came floating down on the Washington field, four mighty motors idling and muttering, as though anxious to blare out and show these ground-moored people just how powerful a sky engine can be.

The ship was single-winged. Its great hull was as flat as the head of a seal. Its double-rigged tail surfaces swished back and forth as Smoke's hand decreed a slip to kill speed.

Sailing as lightly as a drifting, settling feather, the sea boat/land plane came to rest on the field, dwarfing everything in sight.

Girard paced restlessly, looking at the mammoth ship each time he turned. His eyes were like glass reflecting fire.

"Smith!" cried Girard. "That Super-Comet! Where in the name of heaven did Smoke Burnham get money enough together to get that?"

Smith started to say yes and then blinked and scratched his head. Claw marks were long, narrow and red on the back of his hand.

"I'll have to change plans!" exclaimed Girard. "I'll have to wire South America about this! That thing can make three hundred miles an hour without straining a strut!"

"You got the plane, haven't you, sir?"

"The plane? Certainly I've got the plane. But what's that got to do with it? If I turned it over to the government, Smoke Burnham could prove ownership! Smith, something will *have* to be done about it!"

"What's the matter with what we figured out, sir? You see that they get lost down there in the jungle, and then you send out a rescue party, paying for it. The circulation would jump, sir. I don't think Burnham will—"

Girard's eyes snapped. His voice came thin and sharp:

"To hell with what you think! Ah, there come the LeFarges. Good afternoon, Mrs. LeFarge. Look at these brave boys lined up here, ready to do or die for the progress of aviation. Ready to dare the jungles and the seas and the high ranges, so that the torch may be carried on. . . ."

Smoke Burnham walked down the steps from the door of the gigantic ship and stared back up at the hull. "Holy gee!" he said reverently. "She flies like a gull."

Alex nodded and seated himself on a lowered wheel. "Rides nice. Seems too bad for you to have to be in that office all by yourself, Smoke. You'll rattle around like dice in a cup."

Smoke's deep blue eyes gave Alex a quiet study. "You mean you aren't going?"

"Who said I was going?"

"You are this time, Alex."

"But who'll handle the publicity?"

Smoke shrugged. "The printed page once more! You can fly, Alex, and you're the copilot of this ship. It will be a nice jaunt for you in spite of those eighteen thousand miles."

Alex sighed, studied Smoke. After a little, he said, "All right. I'll be able to handle the publicity through the radio. But I thought maybe you'd need someone to look for you when you disappeared somewhere."

"Girard will take care of that."

"Will he? I thought maybe he was just going to get you lost. You look funny, Smoke. Like you've got something under your yellow scalp. What is it?"

Smoke turned away and looked over the multitude of waiting wings. They were of every description and nationality. Two-, three-, four-motored ships. Monoplanes and biplanes. Amphibians and land planes. And over in the Potomac seaplanes were floating.

For once, the weather was nice. Neither hot nor cold, too bright nor too dark. The Potomac mirrored a few clouds—great white cotton tufts in the blue.

The pilots were standing about the blocked-off portion of the operations office. The white building seemed small beside these ships. Faces were looking restlessly toward Girard and toward men who wore ribbons on their faultless coats.

The interest in these officials was as sharp as a prop blade. In their hands rested the fate of some thirty ships and some sixty men. These officials were launching wings across the skies—and these officials knew little else than that planes were sometimes dangerous, as though that made any difference. Pilots weren't human, anyway.

A tight huddle of men in morning coats and spats, ringed round by men in slacks on whose heads rested helmets and goggles.

Beefy, red faces in direct contrast to lean, brown jaws and quick, observant eyes.

A handful of officials, handing out mimeographed orders to palms without looking at the receivers' faces.

Silk hats versus weather-stained leather. The silk hats were launching sixty men into the unknown and semiknown. And the silk hats would sit in easy chairs, with a printed page to tell them what happened to these sixty. In an easy chair, while men rode high to far horizons.

Beefy red faces would be crammed with ham and eggs and caviar, or whatever beefy red faces eat to make them red, while the brown jaws sucked at lukewarm coffee from a battered thermos and tried to swallow stale, dry sandwiches, eating with one hand on a stick and one eye staring into a black door from which there is no returning.

For a printed page? For a vision of stacked bills? For speed? For adventure? For sport?

The answers were not written on the quiet tan faces. In the light gray eyes. They were quiet, these men, while official voices were loud. They waited, these pilots, to step away from pomp into the clean skyways.

A Pan Am pilot, veteran of the jungles, the seas, the storms, drew Smoke Burnham to one side and looked into Smoke's still face with something like sympathy. He knew, that Pan Am man.

"Smoke," he said, smiling, "don't fly your flippers off. A pair of wings is handy down there."

"Sure," said Smoke. "Think the Super-Comet will stand the upcurrents in the Andes?"

"Maybe the ship will," said the Pan Am veteran. His eyes were seeing great reaches of brown peaks lathered with white driving snow. Altitudes where a man couldn't breathe. He was feeling his ship lose a thousand feet in a second, gain two thousand before he could jerk her level. He was feeling the howling power of wind glancing off mountainsides. Wind with the velocity of light.

"I guess it will," he amended.

"How about Colombia?" asked Smoke.

The Pan Am pilot saw hammering rain, silver streaks through a striving prop. He felt the sticky, scorching quality of the swamps.

The older pilot smiled.

"It's a good country, Smoke. Kind of warm."

"And Chile?" said Smoke, cracking a smile.

"Nitrate looks like ice," commented the veteran. And the sun went up to a hundred and thirty and you died before you could crawl across the sun-blasted plains for help.

"Tell me," said Smoke, "did they ever discover the headwaters of the Amazon?"

The veteran shook his head. "A fellow says he did. Said he navigated a party up to the headwaters. Took them months and months to get upstream. And they traveled fast." He saw the shimmering streak which was the headwaters. He had seen it once. Had circled over it and had gone on. Charles Burgess was down there, somewhere. Never thought he'd die, Charley. Chance to get out if you had the equipment, the boats, the guns.

The veteran smiled. "You're wise to all that, Smoke. Why

ask me? I can't tell you a thing about it. They're calling your name."

Smoke turned and saw that an official was holding some papers toward him.

"Your clearance papers," explained Girard. "If you come down anywhere, you'll need them."

"Thanks," Smoke replied. Somewhere near, a shutter clicked and registered Girard's hail-fellow smile. Smoke went back to the Super-Comet amphibian.

Mel King was standing under the wing, dwarfed by it. She wore a bright blue dress, Russian style, with silver cartridge cases edged in gold braid. A saucy Russian hat was perched on the side of her head. All in all, she looked quite gay, and Smoke was heartened.

But, unfortunately, the color of her mood and dress were identical. She turned to Smoke, her eyes misty, her hand clutching a damp bit of lace.

"You're really . . . really going, Smoke?"

"Right," said Smoke, steeling himself for a flood of tears. He loved her too much to watch her cry. It was hard enough just standing there looking at her, wanting to put his arms around her and tell her that it was all right, that the jungles wouldn't get him.

She stepped back a foot at a time. "Then . . . then, Smoke, this is goodbye."

"Sure it is, Mel. But only for eight or nine or ten days."

"It's goodbye for always, Smoke. I . . . I can't hold you. You love flying more than you love me. I can't be with you—in your heart, I mean—unless—"

Smoke was stepping forward. His yellow hair was pulled awry by his helmet. His gloved hands were open, relaxed. His shoulders were very square. A small smile was playing across his face as lightning plays over a field.

He gripped her wrist and jerked her to him. Her face went blank with surprise. The handkerchief fluttered down to the gravel.

Pointing at the door, Smoke said, "Get in!"

"But I've seen the ship. Let me go!"

"Get in!" Smoke repeated. "You're off for South America. Perhaps I can teach you, show you why . . . why I fly. Get in!"

He lifted her bodily up to the cabin floor and thrust her back into an upholstered chair among piles of equipment. Patty raised a sleepy head from the rear of the compartment, looked at Mel, and then went back to sleep.

Smoke slid under the control wheel and gunned the engines. Mel knew that a scream was a whisper beside the bellow of two thousand horses. She sat very still, watching Smoke's throttle hand. . . .

CHAPTER SEVEN

Down on Jungle or River?

EIGHTEEN thousand miles on a map. You can stand back and look at it. You can read the curving names of the countries at a glance. You can run your finger along the route in less than five seconds.

But that isn't traveling over it, inch by inch, mile by mile. That isn't looking down at it and seeing that it's hard and big, and filled with strange things. That isn't battling its elements, its people, its geography.

The Andes stood out like sentinels against the sky. Bleak, bitter, without a single relieving green spray. Snow lay heavily upon them. Clouds lay like beards against the steep sides. But the tops were bare and rugged. Barren of snow. Barren of clouds. Right-angled reaches of land which would never be of any use except as a barrier between the east and west coasts of South America.

Beyond them lay Brazil, jungle, uncharted rivers. But here were the Andes.

The Super-Comet bored toward the icy peaks, engines booming. Smoke Burnham's hands were steady on the control wheel and his eyes were steady on the panel. From time to time a flurry of snow struck the shield before his face, momentarily blotting out the world. Then the sun would shine again.

Alex Montague was sitting at the radio, phones glued to his gray locks, his face intent on the dial.

The cabin of the mammoth amphibian was roomy, and it was furnished with plush and leather.

Mel King's eyes were steady on Smoke's back. Something like respect, something more than admiration, was mirrored on her face.

She had seen Smoke play tag with line squalls all the way across the Caribbean. She had seen him coast down to the water's edge to pick up his drift from a steamer's funnel. She had seen him sit there, hour in, hour out, hands on that wheel, relieved only occasionally by Alex.

She had watched the reflection of his face in the shield. His beard was making headway, but, like his hair, it was yellow and did not show. His shirt was a little torn, perhaps a little dirty. His bare arms were brown, stained by splotches of grease.

Smoke's unjarrable nerves had brought them all the way down South America's west coast, in sight of the mountains, in sight of the sea. He was always ready with a smile when he turned toward her. Then he would remember his work and turn back.

That hasty remembrance of work had always stood like the Andes between them. Flight had kept them apart—and Melanie King was now beginning to suspect that, perhaps, flight was worthwhile. She had flown, yes. But she had never known the steady devotion of a man to his work. She had never appreciated that there was anything but danger in that work.

• MAN-KILLERS OF THE AIR •

Alex was speaking and his voice was clearly audible in the soundproof cabin. "Hagner is down."

Smoke turned his head a little but did not take his eyes from the looming mountains. "Where?"

"Between Panama and Ecuador. Maybe along the equator. Eight hours overdue into Chile. No reports along the line."

Smoke remembered the ranges up there, that chill plateau paradoxically along the supposedly hottest belt in the world. No place to land.

"Tough," said Smoke. He took his wheel hand away long enough to light a cigarette. The Super-Comet flew serenely on. The compass shifted a fraction of a point.

"No further word from Jonesy," said Alex. "They've patrolled the Caribbean for two days."

"I said he hit a squall."

Mel came up the aisle and stood at Alex's side. "You mean he's dead?"

Alex nodded, still staring at the dial.

"That's the fifth," she said in a low voice. She was watching the Andes come at them at four and a half miles a minute. The tan ground below seemed to creep.

"Yeah," said Smoke, through lips which clenched his fag. "Inferior equipment." Snow bombarded them again and he nosed up, increasing his angle of climb.

"Aren't . . . aren't you worried, Alex?" said Mel.

Alex glanced up at her. "Worried? Why should you and I worry, with that boy under the gun?"

"But," replied Mel, "there was something mysterious about the way our broadcaster went out on us before we hit Chile."

"You mean those smashed tubes? Some peon monkeying with it, that's all—when we were putting in that change of gas." Alex was thinking about Girard. Girard didn't want them to come back. "Forget it, Mel."

Patty got up, stretched with a glance at the Andes, turned around in the leather seat and was then promptly claimed by the sandman.

"Follow Patty's advice," said Alex. "She knows enough to trust Smoke."

No other plane in sight. Nothing but mountains in front and foothills beneath. Nothing but snow flurries, and they would be gone when they built another thousand feet of altitude. The superchargers on the engines were yowling louder than the motors themselves, sending in the required oxygen. Air was getting thin up there.

"Who's ahead of us?" said Smoke.

"Bradshaw and Klein," replied Alex. "We're second."

"We'll gain that over these mountains."

"Why so?" said Alex.

"We won't try for the peaks. We'll take the pass that I've got marked on this chart."

"Not afraid of this last batch of gas?"

"Why should I be? I strained it."

"She doesn't seem to have the soup, Smoke."

"You're dreaming!"

The foothills began to ascend below, as though the Super-Comet was coming down. However, a glance at the angle-of-climb indicator stated that they were only a few points below the stalling mark. Two thousand horses drank greedily of the tanks. Four whirling clubs shoved onward through the thinning air.

The Andes were there with them.

A peak reared up to the south—Mount Tupungato, 22,310 feet high. They were far below the summit, diminutive in a colossal world of chasms, ranges, mighty rivers.

A gust of wind struck the underside of the left wing. The ship careened drunkenly. Mel snatched at a chair and buckled on her safety belt. Another gust caught them amidships. They sank like an express elevator. A downdraft battered them back, like a smashing fist. A side current bore them relentlessly at a mountainside, hundreds of feet a second, until it seemed inevitable that they would crash.

Smoke, still puffing on the cigarette, shot the throttles all the way on and banked.

They rocketed straight for a blank wall. A lift caught them and shot them over the top of the ridge. A downdraft sucked them into the ravine beyond.

Mel's head whirled in a giddy world where everything was suddenly very close at hand, everything, including death. The Caribbean squalls, the heat, everything paled beside this.

At three hundred miles an hour, Smoke shot them down the ravine. He charged one side as though bent on suicide.

"Here goes a bump!" he cried.

The ship staggered. The wings dipped and shivered. They soared up, up, up, lifted bodily into the incredibly blue sky.

Mel's head whirled in a giddy world where everything was suddenly very close at hand, everything, including death.

Smoke's words suddenly struck home to Mel. He knew what he was doing. He wasn't flying blind. He knew where the upcurrents would be, where the downdrafts would hit them. He knew how to make the ricocheting wind help them.

A mountain was under them and a mountain was above them. They were mere Gullivers in Brobdingnag, and the Andes were the giants. They were a baby's toy ship sent heartlessly into a hurricane.

Mel looked up into the shield and saw the reflection of Smoke's face. It startled her to know that he was smiling. She had expected to see white knuckles and set jaw, and instead she saw a smile of pure pleasure.

For an instant it annoyed her, that smile. Then, when they sank down into another ravine and soared up the far side, she found the heart to smile with him. After all, it *was* fun, if you didn't think too much about what would happen if an engine failed, if a wing buckled, if a sudden cloud enwrapped them. . . .

Like a scrap of paper in a typhoon they were thrown through the mountain-studded sky. Three hundred miles an hour. Five miles a minute. Four hundred and forty feet a second. A block and a half a second!

The Indians had *toiled* over these mountains, painful rods an hour, deluged by tumbling rocks of an avalanche, hacked down by the arrows of an enemy, plodding, plodding, plodding.

Two thousand horses. Five miles a minute. Ravines were under them and gone in the space of seconds. Mountains fled to the rear.

Abruptly the air was still. The throbbing motors dropped a note in their strident song of unbridled power.

Mel sat up, fearful that they were about to crash, that something had gone wrong.

Ahead, far ahead and below, lay green, flat plains. Smooth, soothing to the eye. Unlimited. The pampas of the Argentine!

Smoke turned as he glided down to a more breathable level. The dead cigarette was still dangling from his lips. "Have a nice roller-coaster ride?" he asked her.

At Rio, gliding up a bay of the purest turquoise, they bumped the dock and climbed out, thankful for a chance to stretch their legs.

"Go ahead," said Smoke. "Get something hot to eat. I'm going to check these engines."

Alex started to hang back, and then knew that he would only be in the way. He followed Mel up a smooth, paved street and tried to realize that they were in Brazil, in the southern hemisphere, some twelve thousand miles on their way.

An official stood below the wing and talked in broken English up at Smoke. "You skirt the coast, see? You follow the beach. That way you do not have to fight the jungle."

"Rats!" said Smoke. "I'm going straight across to Panama."

"I know of no rats," said the official, swarthy and braided, and puzzled.

Mechanics were pouring gasoline into the tanks, drum after drum. Straining it through chamois. They cared but little how much gas they placed in the ship, how many thousands of gallons. Some Americano with more money than brains had said he would pay the bill. Some Americano named Girard. And all these planes would get their gas. No matter how many thousand gallons. They had never heard of Girard.

That is, no one but Manuel had ever heard of Girard, and Manuel was not speaking about it. He was standing up on the wing, watching the fluid gurgle into the wing tanks. And with each barrel he would drop a handful of white powder into the open hole. But before he dropped the white powder, he looked about to see that no one noticed. Especially that Americano there, tinkering with the motors. Americanos have a way of being fatal when angered.

Alex and Mel came back, laughing. Mel had a balloon she had purchased in a very Spanish toy store, and she was bouncing it on her palm as she walked.

Patty stood in the doorway of the cabin and watched her. Seeing the cheetah, the mechanics drew away, wondering why a man should want to carry a jaguar about with him. These Americanos! They carried jaguars and played with balloons. But then, a beautiful lady might as well amuse herself while she lived. Aviators and jungle . . .

Patty watched Mel come up the steps. Standing back, pretending not to notice, Patty yawned elaborately. Suddenly the balloon bobbed within a foot of her nose. She struck.

The balloon exploded.

Patty yowled, jumped far back into the cabin, and sat down, wrapping her tail about her legs with a very injured air. Patty did not like to have people laugh at her.

The Super-Comet taxied out into the stream, headed into the wind, and two thousand horses howled as she took the air.

"We're heading west of north," explained Smoke, munching on the sandwich Mel had brought him along with a thermos of particularly vile Spanish coffee.

"Across the jungles," commented Alex.

The plane roared on a thousand feet above the crouching, spraddling trees. Mangroves, coffee bushes, rice paddies, tobacco and sugar cane whipped away from front to rear.

Night came like a light bulb suddenly turned off. After that there was only darkness and the roar of engines and the lighted panel in front of Smoke's face. . . .

Mel dozed fitfully, lulled by the engines. Once she woke long enough to hear Alex say, "Connelly's down in the Andes. Banner spotted the wreckage." Then she was back in New York running her roadster full speed down an express highway.

Somebody was shouting, "Wake up!" But the car kept right on going and she couldn't see anything except an instrument panel.

"Wake up!" cried Smoke again.

Terror clutched at her. Smoke looked so shadowy and unreal sitting before that panel. "What's wrong?"

Not until then did she know that the engines were dead. Wind was sighing in the struts. Had they reached Panama again? No, Panama was miles from there, thousands of miles from Brazil.

And they were going down on soundless wings to a waiting jungle from which there was never any escape.

Stars were bright in the ebon sky. Nothing moved. Only the wind in their struts. A motor caught and then died once more.

Alex was hanging out the door. Something was in his hand. The world turned white below under the icy sputter of a flare.

"Anything?" cried Smoke.

"Reflection of something!"

"Water?"

"I don't know. Circle!"

Another flare went over. The landing lights were pale white streaks out before them, reaching, reaching, trying to contact the forgotten jungles, trying to find water, a clear field.

Smoke, eyes straining into the black wall of silence, juggled the sluggish wheel. Going down. Down into what? Seven planes were out of it. Six would be heard no more. Would they be the eighth? He tried to jab the four throttles, but the engines were gone now. He had known they would go, an hour before, when they had first started to cough.

Four engines, all gone. Funny to think of Girard's hand reaching out of the far northern country down into the thickest of Brazil.

For headlines. For circulation. For a ship which would stop that widely published threat of Japan. For the prestige of giving the government that plane.

For a fleeting instant Smoke wondered why he was here. Was it for the printed page? The speed? Or the sport?

The retreating wall which would suddenly be replaced by trees seemed to darken. Alex was hanging on, looking down, tossing flares like hand grenades as though to drive away the menace of trees. The fuselage flares were long gone, lost back there when the engines had first started to miss and chatter in their gas-starved bellies.

"Water?" begged Smoke.

"Can't see," said Alex.

Mel watched Patty pace restlessly down the aisle. Patty knew that something was wrong. Perhaps Patty, if she lived, would soon be back in her element, the jungle. But then, no one survives a head-on smash into trees. Branches would bite greedily into them, rip them apart. And the wreckage would be swallowed, soon to be covered by sinuous creepers. Another toll. Perhaps the eighth.

The printed page. The speed. The sport. Girard. A legion driven onward by spurs they could not name. A tan-faced, lean-jawed legion facing a wide, clear sky, their clear eyes unafraid.

Whispering struts. A murmur of sound which was the jungle. A mangrove came magically toward them, deceptively soft and inviting.

"Water?" pleaded Smoke.

Alex didn't answer. He came back into the cabin, sat down and fastened his safety belt. He picked up a cushion and held it in front of his face. Mel hurried to follow his example.

Jungle. A thousand miles from nowhere. Months on foot. And if you were hurt, then you were lost. Living on monkey meat. Drinking water from stagnant pools. Listening to the shriek of a jaguar and the calls of strange birds. Patty was narrow-eyed and tense. The odors of land below were stirring strange things in her dun-colored breast.

"Water!" cried Smoke, his voice hollow and weirdly loud in the silence of whistling wind.

The black strip was under their hull. The big amphibian veered to the right, wings at four o'clock. The landing lights reached out with probing fingers, turning the black strip into a pale, iridescent green.

Trees bounded them. The ship sideslipped, came around again. The hull struck with a dull crack.

Spray rose in black plumes all about them, drenching them, but they welcomed it. The hull slid through the pale green fluid as though it was greased.

Smoke jockeyed the plane with deft, swift fingers. Gradually their speed diminished and then they were bobbing gently on the rippling wide reaches of the Rio Solimões, close to the Colombian border.

Smoke was instantly out of the cabin, climbing up to the motors on the wing. Alex handed him a flashlight and a wrench. Mel stared in front of her, seeing nothing, weak from reaction.

Smoke's voice was cheerful. "These jets are all plugged with camphor! Listen. Get some buckets and drain all tanks into the empty center tank!"

It was odd, hearing his voice out of that hot, steaming night. Mel rose and rummaged until she found the buckets. Then she stepped out along the hull and met Alex.

"We need something to strain it with," said Alex. "We've got to clean God knows how many hundred gallons of gas, while Smoke clears those jets. We need some silk."

Her face in the light of his flash grew a little red. Then she went back into the cabin and came forth presently with something silk to strain a few hundred gallons of the fluid that would lift them out of this steaming swamp. After that, the gurgle of gasoline blended with the ripple of the stream, punctuated by the clanking of wrenches up on the wing, where Smoke worked feverishly to repair their maimed power plants. Mel was smiling, her eyes alight with a fire of resolve. She had been strengthened by something she could not name. By the sound of the wrenches? By the knowledge that they were far from the world? By the cries of the jungle at night?

Her arms were weary when the motors were running again. She was soaked with gasoline and her head felt light from the fumes. But she stood beside Smoke as he taxied out to clear water and started the plunging run which would whip them into the air.

After that she dozed once more, waking when they reached the cold gray harbor of Colón. She felt older, wiser, cleaner than she had when they had first touched this water. Importantly, cold in the brisk wind of a tropical morning, she stood by a tank and watched to see that nothing but strained gas was poured into the ship.

Then the Central American nations and Mexico and its high plateaus. A sweeping expanse of rough green and tan. Peons in the fields, plowing with yoked bull teams. Squat towns, all alike.

The dust and cries of Mexico City, and on again toward California.

Alex was at the radio, listening, his head bent forward, his eyes unseeing. Smoke's yellow hair whipped as the wind rippled through a partly opened port.

"Five ahead of us," said Alex, as though talking to himself.

"Who?"

"Doesn't matter. The tenth ship is down."

"Five ahead of us, eh?" said Smoke.

It seemed to Mel that they flew forever before they reached Lindbergh Field in San Diego. And then she felt as though someone had handed her a new life. It was so good to see honest American faces, to hear the hearty swearing of hurrying mechanics.

A weather bureau man was thrusting papers at Smoke through the door. "All closed in from Mississippi east. And getting thicker. Better pause awhile. No use killing yourself, Burnham."

"Did the others go through?"

"Sure they did."

"You don't see me pulling any throttles, do you?"

The weatherman laughed and went away. And then they were flying in the dusk, headed east, with a tail wind helping them to attain a speed of five miles a minute.

The Super-Comet charged toward a gray horizon with renewed life. Airmail beacons were blinking dots down on the carpet of earth—that ever-unrolling carpet.

The fog hit them before they came to the big river. It curled through their struts and props and wrapped them in cotton batting. It blanketed the world, hid it from sight. They seemed to remain suspended, unmoving.

Smoke flew blind, not watching the fog. Only a few instruments on a panel, telling them that they were still right side up, still doing five miles a minute.

Smoke shut off the wing lights, and the fog went black. He turned them on again. White cotton was preferable to nothing at all.

Alex was tense at the radio. "They're still ahead of us," he said.

"She's doing her best," said Smoke. He was thinking about that note for fifty thousand. The note for two thousand. The hospital and hotel bills. The Mystery Ship and Girard. It was suddenly very close to him. The payoff would come high.

With clean gas pouring into them, the engines were doing better. With damp air roaring through the superchargers, they were straining themselves to the limit, racking their cylinders and crankcases.

Smoke pushed all four throttles up their tridents until they would go no further. Synchronization was gone. The engines were pounding against one another in a discordant bellow.

CHAPTER EIGHT

While Groundlings Fume

THREE o'clock in the morning is early for a newspaper magnate to be up and around. Perhaps his reporters have been on the job for twenty-four hours straight. Perhaps the editors are still hunched over their desks, fighting off sleep to put out the noon edition.

But Paul Harrison Girard wasn't worried about his editors. He was thinking in terms of circulation, advertising, stacked bills. Today would be a big day. Sales would be up. All over the United States people would want to know how these pilots were coming out.

It was dark on the field—dark, but noisy. An announcer from a broadcast chain was pulling Girard's overcoat sleeve. "Can't get any reports. They hear planes, but they can't identify them to the west. I don't know who's ahead."

"We'll know soon enough," said Girard. "What was the last report? Where was Burnham?"

"Fifth west of the Mississippi. But there's been a crash since then. And people are saying that pilots can't see this port." He looked up at the fog, worried. It was impossible to see the Pilot's Club from the operations office.

The announcer lit a cigarette with shaking fingers. "Maybe they won't land on this field. Maybe they'll hit Bolling or someplace else."

"It isn't disqualifying," Girard grunted.

Two men from the War Department came up, chins deep in upturned collars of their trench coats. "You say you've got a surprise for us, Girard."

Girard smiled, and his jowls shook as he jerked his thumb at the line. "See that ship out there? That's a two-place, all-metal pursuit job. Fastest thing in the air. That's my answer to invasion's threat, gentlemen."

The War Department men nodded. "We know. We've been looking it over. Burnham developed it, didn't he?"

"That's right. And now I've purchased it to give to you."

"To *give* to us. My God, man, that's colossal! That's the greatest thing you've ever done. You mean that our Army pilots can actually have planes like that?"

Girard chuckled. "I thought you'd be pleased. We'll have a formal presentation just as soon as this race ceases to be front-page news."

"Got to keep up circulation, huh?"

Unabashed, Girard nodded. "Damned right. Listen! There's a motor!"

A field official bawled, "Blink your landing lights!"

The hum of the motor died out. The ship was gone.

"False alarm," said an Army man. "It must have been an airliner."

Minutes passed. Men smoked cigarette after cigarette, paced up and down. The crowd that had turned out stood silent and chilled along the edges of the field, their heads up, listening, trying to see through the wet, clinging fog that bounded them.

"Another engine!" bawled an announcer.

The pilot was gunning his motor. The muffled *brrrr-up, brrr-up, burrr-up!* came to the groundlings like the far-off coughing of a giant.

Something like a landing gear appeared through the white sky. The landing lights were on, steadily, glaring into the mist like great eyes.

A red speed ship greased down to the runway and rolled to a stop just clear of the line. A concerted roar went up.

It was Raymond! Girard's own entry!

Girard chuckled. Well, this wasn't going to cost him any fifty thousand dollars after all. It was better than he had hoped. He went up and helped the tired pilot out of his red ship.

The announcer slapped Raymond on the back and shoved a mike under his nose. People surged toward them, cheering, all talking at once.

Raymond, winner of the International Air Derby! The greatest pilot in the skyways!

Girard was talking into a mike, telling the world how proud he was, forgetting to mention that strewn wreckage on another continent. Forgetting the others of the tanned legion. Mentioning the newspapers again and again and again. As many times as the announcer would permit. And the announcer was not listening closely.

The announcer had turned and was staring out at the fringe of the crowd. Something familiar had caught his eye through the fog.

A striding figure. A hand on a leash. The soft, prowling gait of a cheetah!

It was Smoke Burnham!

"Wait!" cried the announcer into the mike. "There's something wrong, people. It looks as though Smoke Burnham—"

Smoke was there, standing beside Girard, his path cleared by Patty.

Smoke was grinning through a coating of grease and whiskers. His eyes were hollow, but they were laughing. His yellow hair was bared to the chill mist.

"I landed at Bolling Field fifteen minutes ago," said Smoke to the questions of excited officials. "Didn't you hear my motors through this pea soup?"

"Sure," said the announcer. "We heard them."

"I saw a clear patch over there and I thought maybe I might land on the crowd if I tried it here. For once, Bolling was clearer than this place."

Girard was snorting and puffing. His eyes were as large and as protruding as golf balls. "You . . . you . . . you can't get away with this, Burnham. I'll check you up and show that you're—"

Another official came through the crowd, crying, "Smoke Burnham landed at Bolling ten minutes before Raymond got here! I just called—"

After that everything overlapped and became entangled. Mikes, faces, cameras, reporters. The roaring of a thousand voices. The circling *brr-up, brrr-up* of landing ships.

Almost an hour later, the two Army men found time to step between Girard, the microphone and Smoke Burnham. "We understand, Burnham, that Girard bought this plane from you to present to the Army. That right? We don't want any errors."

Girard stared about him as though looking for cover. Smoke was smiling. "That's right. He paid me three hundred thousand dollars for the construction rights. Only he forgot to give me the check. You'd better write it now, Girard."

There was no cover for Girard, no escape from the spot he was in.

"But I . . . I just gave you fifty thousand for the race, Burnham! And I'm building you that plant twice as big as the one you had. You damned—"

The Army men were startled. They frowned at Girard wonderingly. Girard caught the look in their eyes. Face was everything. Everything!

"Just joking, Burnham," he said. "Just giving you a run for your money." He smiled loosely, somewhat sickly, and placed his arm around Burnham's shoulders. Patty sat down on one of Girard's feet, and he swallowed as she looked up, adoringly, into his face.

"We'll get a picture," said Smoke, "of you writing that check. Hey, newsreel! Camera and mike over here!"

Girard fumbled for his checkbook and scribbled the required paper. He waved it before the flickering lens, which found light enough in the dawn to photograph such a large sum of money.

"We'll talk about the plant later in the day," said Smoke, taking the check. "I've got that in a contract, you know."

"Yes, yes," agreed Girard, and backed swiftly away before Smoke thought of anything else.

Smoke grinned.

Alex was there. "Listen, Smoke! I've sold advertising to a toothpaste company and a cigarette company and—"

"Did you get the money?"

"You bet," said Alex, patting his pocket.

Mel forgot that her blue dress was stained with gasoline and that her nose knew no powder. She was beautiful just the same. Her eyes made her beautiful as she looked at Smoke.

"Smoke, I want to tell you. I want to tell you now that I understand."

"I'm glad," said Smoke gently.

"I understand what makes you fly. What makes you take those chances." Her face was shining from an inner light as she gripped his tattered sleeve. "I understand, Smoky dear. It's not the publicity, it's . . . it's . . ."

"Never mind," said Smoke. "The publicity. The sport. The speed. The thrill of it. The exhilaration of contest. I don't know what it is, so why should you? It's . . . it's down here, Mel." He touched his heart and then reached out and covered the place with Mel.

Patty smiled a feline smile and fell to licking grease-stained paws.

Story Preview

NOW that you've just ventured through one of the captivating tales in the Stories from the Golden Age collection by L. Ron Hubbard, turn the page and enjoy a preview of *Sabotage in the Sky*. Join Bill Trevillian, an ace pilot who tests new fighter planes for the Allied Forces and is competing with another company to get a multi-million-dollar aircraft contract. Covert enemy agents have tampered with the new warbird, deliberately marking it for failure regardless of the cost.

Sabotage in the Sky

ERICH VON STRAUB resembled very little the stiff Nazi officer who had, so recently, clicked his heels and bowed shortly to the Minister of the Air in Berlin. Then his manner had been perfectly Prussian.

The Minister of the Air in Berlin had said, "Colonel, according to your record, you studied aeronautical engineering in the United States and you speak the language and know the country. We have a great deal of faith in you. I have had you report here to inform you that you are leaving, via Italy, with properly forged passports and birth certificates, for the United States."

"Yes, sir," said von Straub.

"The English and the French are depending on the planes of the United States to achieve their air supremacy. Already we have a sufficient number of agents at work in United States aircraft plants, but they are watched so closely that they can do very little. You, Colonel, have always been a man of resource and intelligence."

"Thank you, sir."

"You understand that unless this flow of superior planes is at least hampered, we cannot long hope to continue victorious in the sky. We believe that the best method of hampering this flow of planes is to influence English and French opinion of them. Soon we will have the Messerschmitt 118D for pursuit. It has been brought to us that the United States has, in experimental condition, the one plane which will defeat the Messerschmitt 118D. One other plane is nearly equal to it. The British and French are trying to buy these two types of ship. If those planes convince the British and French that they are superior, the manufacture of the Messerschmitt 118D will be reduced in importance. But, Colonel, you are a resourceful man.

"We are not tampering with our production of the Messerschmitt 118D. We will depend upon you to keep the British and French from buying either of these two American planes and then, because 118D is a secret we will maintain with our lives, we will suddenly be able to take over the sky from the English, sweep their isles, down their retaliating bombers, and so bring victory to our glorious cause.

"If you can arrange to convince the English and French that these two American planes are neither safe nor fast, you will find yourself a hero in your own land. Failing that, you will deliver to us a complete plane of each type. Ample funds are at your disposal. The lives of your brother officers depend upon you, so work well!"

"Heil Hitler!" von Straub piously said, turning sharply and marching away.

But Erich von Straub, a man of resource and intelligence, did not at all resemble Albert Straud who had, very recently, been hired as an aviation mechanic by Beryl-Cannard Airlines. Albert Straud was obviously a Teuton, but then so are a large percent of the employees of all aircraft companies in the United States. His blond hair was curly and his eyes were mild and of an innocent blue; he was of medium stature and only passingly handsome; his bearing had no suggestion of the military, but leaned rather into careless ease. He was cheerful and conversational and helpful and, in fact, lived up completely to the fine letters of recommendation he had brought—letters which had been taken from a Boeing man who had somehow managed to get himself killed in an automobile crash.

He stood just now, this Albert Straud, on the apron of the BCA plant's second hangar and scanned, with a fellow employee, the murky heights of the southern sky—for BCA is only thirty miles from Washington, DC, and shares Washington, DC's climate.

There was a flash of silver up there and a powerful engine became loud so suddenly that it sounded more like an explosion than an approaching plane. Abruptly the roar stopped. The silver became a low-wing monoplane, stabbing down at the field. And nearly every man on the BCA property froze, drop-jawed and unbreathing.

Planes landing there were too common to be remarked. But two things were different about this ship. One was that it was coming in upside down, and the other, that it probably contained one Bill Trevillian, absent from these parts for nearly four years.

Straight down the runway streaked the ship, the pilot seemingly wholly undisturbed by this reversal of the average state of scenery. And then, almost at the stalling point, when it seemed that he must inevitably crash, he snap rolled! And when the plane's landing gear was under it where it should have been all the time, the wheels were also being rotated by an instantaneous contact with earth.

There was a furious geyser of dust at the runway's end and the field was full of a joyous bellow of power—and the silver ship nearly took off again, headed toward the hangars. Another cloud, then the sputter of a cut motor, and there sat the plane, parked neatly on the line, in between two fighting planes, almost touching wings on either side.

"Well, well, well!" said Albert Straud. "I have not seen that since the great Udet. Any idea who the pilot might be?"

His companion, a stocky fellow with a wise eye and a mouth full of tobacco, namely Greasy Hannagan, spat and drawled, "You evidently ain't never seen Bill Trevillian before, buddy. Him and Udet used to pick handkerchiefs out of the breast pockets of each other's Sunday suits with their wing tips."

"Bill Trevillian? Oh, yes. The racing pilot. I should like to know him."

"You'll know him all right, buddy. You and me is goin' to be his repair crew. He's up here from Mexico to take charge of the BCA 41 Pursuit."

"Ah. So they've been waiting for him before they tried it again."

"Yeah. They been waiting for him. Hello, Bill, you old scatter-wit!"

"'Lo, Greasy. You wouldn't be putting on weight, would you?"

"Hell," said Greasy, "what's the difference? Ain't like it used to be, conserving the payload. How you been?"

Bill Trevillian had eased half out of the pit and sat now on the turtleback, his long, booted legs dangling, while he untangled himself from his radio helmet and oxygen mask. He was good-looking in a sleepy sort of way, very tall, very languid, always looking for something upon which to lean his obviously weary soul. Down in his eyes there lay a watchful spark of humor, and upon his lips there always lingered the ghost of his last smile and the beginning of the next.

> To find out more about *Sabotage in the Sky* and how you can obtain your copy, go to www.goldenagestories.com.

Glossary

STORIES FROM THE GOLDEN AGE *reflect the words and expressions used in the 1930s and 1940s, adding unique flavor and authenticity to the tales. While a character's speech may often reflect regional origins, it also can convey attitudes common in the day. So that readers can better grasp such cultural and historical terms, uncommon words or expressions of the era, the following glossary has been provided.*

aileron: a hinged flap on the trailing edge of an aircraft wing, used to control banking movements.

amphibian: an airplane designed for taking off from and landing on both land and water.

Andes: a mountain range that extends the length of the western coast of South America.

Bolling: Bolling Field; located in southwest Washington, DC and officially opened in 1918, it was named in honor of the first high-ranking air service officer killed in World War I. Bolling served as a research and testing ground for new aviation equipment and its first mission provided aerial defense of the capital.

camphor: a tough, gummy, volatile, aromatic crystalline compound obtained especially from the wood and bark of the camphor tree.

cheetah: also called a hunting leopard. A long-legged,

• GLOSSARY •

swift-running wild cat of Africa and southwest Asia, having tawny, black-spotted fur and nonretractile claws. The cheetah is the fastest animal on land and can run short distances at about sixty miles (ninety-six km) per hour.

club: airplane propeller.

Colón: a seaport in Panama at the Atlantic end of the Panama Canal.

cowl: a removable metal covering for an engine, especially an aircraft engine.

crate: an airplane.

cutaway: a man's formal daytime coat, with front edges sloping diagonally from the waist and forming tails at the back.

fag: cigarette.

fins: fixed vertical surfaces at the tail of an aircraft that give stability, and to which the rudders are attached.

foil: airfoil; any surface (such as a wing, propeller blade or rudder) designed to aid in lifting, directing or controlling an aircraft by using the current of air it moves through.

frau: a wife.

G-men: government men; agents of the Federal Bureau of Investigation.

Gullivers in Brobdingnag: refers to a satire, *Gulliver's Travels*, by Jonathan Swift in 1726. Lemuel Gulliver, an Englishman, travels to exotic lands, including Lilliput (where the people are six inches tall), Brobdingnag (where the people are seventy feet tall), and the land of the Houyhnhnms (where horses are the intelligent beings, and humans, called Yahoos, are mute brutes of labor).

• GLOSSARY •

hail-fellow: heartily friendly and congenial.

hunting leopard: another name for cheetah.

jaguar: a large wildcat of Central and South America, closely related to the leopard and having a tawny coat spotted with black rosettes. One of many spotted cats, a jaguar may be mistaken for a leopard or cheetah.

legman: a reporter who gathers information by visiting news sources, or by being present at news events.

Lindbergh Field: now San Diego Airport; opened in 1928, the airport was named after Charles Lindbergh, since San Diego had the honor of being the city where he began the journey that would ultimately become the first solo transatlantic flight. It was also the first federally certified airfield to serve all aircraft types, including seaplanes. It gained international airport status in 1934.

Malacca: the stem of a species of palm, brown in color and often mottled, used for making canes and umbrella handles; named after a town in western Malaysia.

Messerschmitt: a famous German aircraft manufacturer known primarily for its World War II fighter aircraft. In 1927, Willy Messerschmitt joined the company, then known as Bavarian Aircraft Works, as chief designer. He promoted a new lightweight design in which many separate parts were merged into a single reinforced firewall, thereby saving weight and improving performance. The Messerschmitt became a favorite of the German government and in 1938 the company was renamed with Willy Messerschmitt as chairman.

monoplane: an airplane with one sustaining surface or one set of wings.

• GLOSSARY •

morning coats: men's jackets, usually black, cut away at the front below the waist and with a long divided tail, worn on formal occasions as part of morning dress.

Mount Tupungato: a mountain of 22,310 feet (6,804 meters), in the Andes on the Chile-Argentina border east of Santiago, Chile.

newshawk: a newspaper reporter, especially one who is energetic and aggressive.

Nine: Nine Sports; a two-seater sports car produced in Coventry, England from 1932 to 1937. They were a nine-horsepower range of cars, thus giving them the name *Nine,* and could reach a speed of over sixty-six miles per hour with the windscreen lowered flat.

pampas: large treeless plains in South America.

Pan Am: Pan American World Airways, the principal international airline of the United States from the 1930s until it closed its operations in 1991. Originally founded as a seaplane service out of Florida, the airline became a major company credited with many innovations that shaped the international airline industry.

pash: passion.

peon: (Spanish) a farm worker or unskilled laborer; day laborer.

Potomac: a river in the east central United States; it begins in the Appalachian Mountains in West Virginia and flows eastward to the Chesapeake Bay, forming the boundary between Maryland and Virginia.

Prussian: in the manner of a military officer from Prussia. Prussia, a former northern European nation, based much of

• GLOSSARY •

its rule on armed might, stressing rigid military discipline and maintaining one of the most strictly drilled armies in the world.

pylon: a tower marking a turning point in a race among aircraft.

QT, on the: on the quiet; secretly.

Rio Solimões: the name often given to early stretches of the Amazon River.

roadster: an open-top automobile with a single seat in front for two or three persons, a fabric top and either a luggage compartment or a rumble seat in back. A rumble seat is an upholstered exterior seat with a hinged lid that opens to form the back of the seat when in use.

rod: a measure of length; a rod is sixteen and a half feet.

rudder: a device used to steer ships or aircraft. A rudder is a flat plane or sheet of material attached with hinges to the craft's stern or tail. In typical aircraft, pedals operate rudders via mechanical linkages.

rumble: rumble seat; an upholstered exterior seat in the back of a car with a hinged lid that opens to form the back of the seat when in use.

Scheherazade: the female narrator of *The Arabian Nights,* who during one thousand and one adventurous nights saved her life by entertaining her husband, the king, with stories.

shylock: a hard-hearted banker or lender who is concerned only with profit.

slipstream: the airstream pushed back by a revolving aircraft propeller.

• GLOSSARY •

snap rolled: (of an aircraft) quickly rolled about its longitudinal axis while flying horizontally.

soup: added power, especially horsepower.

SP: Sportsman Pilot; aviation journal published in the 1930s.

spats: cloth or leather covers that fit on the top of men's shoes, extending up over the ankles and fastening under the shoes with a strap.

spatted wheels: a structure around the top of the wheels of a fixed airplane landing gear.

struts: supports for a structure such as an aircraft wing, roof or bridge.

swagger coat: a woman's pyramid-shaped coat with a full flared back and usually raglan sleeves (sleeves extending to the collar of a garment instead of ending at the shoulder), first popularized in the 1930s.

swindle sheet: an expense account.

Teuton: a native of Germany or a person of German origin.

toe the mark: to behave properly.

turtleback: the part of the airplane behind the cockpit that is shaped like the back of a turtle.

Udet: Ernst Udet (1896–1941), the second-highest-scoring German flying ace of World War I, with sixty-two victories.

war box: war chest; a fund reserved for a particular purpose.

yellow journalism: journalism that exploits, distorts or exaggerates the news to create sensations and attract readers.

ZT: aircraft designation for an obsolete trainer. *Z* stands for "obsolete" and *T* is the designation for "trainer."

L. Ron Hubbard
in the Golden Age
of Pulp Fiction

*In writing an adventure story
a writer has to know that he is adventuring
for a lot of people who cannot.
The writer has to take them here and there
about the globe and show them
excitement and love and realism.
As long as that writer is living the part of an
adventurer when he is hammering
the keys, he is succeeding with his story.*

*Adventuring is a state of mind.
If you adventure through life, you have a
good chance to be a success on paper.*

*Adventure doesn't mean globe-trotting,
exactly, and it doesn't mean great deeds.
Adventuring is like art.
You have to live it to make it real.*

—L. RON HUBBARD

L. Ron Hubbard and American Pulp Fiction

BORN March 13, 1911, L. Ron Hubbard lived a life at least as expansive as the stories with which he enthralled a hundred million readers through a fifty-year career.

Originally hailing from Tilden, Nebraska, he spent his formative years in a classically rugged Montana, replete with the cowpunchers, lawmen and desperadoes who would later people his Wild West adventures. And lest anyone imagine those adventures were drawn from vicarious experience, he was not only breaking broncs at a tender age, he was also among the few whites ever admitted into Blackfoot society as a bona fide blood brother. While if only to round out an otherwise rough and tumble youth, his mother was that rarity of her time—a thoroughly educated woman—who introduced her son to the classics of Occidental literature even before his seventh birthday.

But as any dedicated L. Ron Hubbard reader will attest, his world extended far beyond Montana. In point of fact, and as the son of a United States naval officer, by the age of eighteen he had traveled over a quarter of a million miles. Included therein were three Pacific crossings to a then still mysterious Asia, where he ran with the likes of Her British Majesty's agent-in-place

• L. RON HUBBARD •

L. Ron Hubbard, left, at Congressional Airport, Washington, DC, 1931, with members of George Washington University flying club.

for North China, and the last in the line of Royal Magicians from the court of Kublai Khan. For the record, L. Ron Hubbard was also among the first Westerners to gain admittance to forbidden Tibetan monasteries below Manchuria, and his photographs of China's Great Wall long graced American geography texts.

Upon his return to the United States and a hasty completion of his interrupted high school education, the young Ron Hubbard entered George Washington University. There, as fans of his aerial adventures may have heard, he earned his wings as a pioneering barnstormer at the dawn of American aviation. He also earned a place in free-flight record books for the longest sustained flight above Chicago. Moreover, as a roving reporter for *Sportsman Pilot* (featuring his first professionally penned articles), he further helped inspire a generation of pilots who would take America to world airpower.

Immediately beyond his sophomore year, Ron embarked on the first of his famed ethnological expeditions, initially to then untrammeled Caribbean shores (descriptions of which would later fill a whole series of West Indies mystery-thrillers). That the Puerto Rican interior would also figure into the future of Ron Hubbard stories was likewise no accident. For in addition to cultural studies of the island, a 1932–33

♦ AMERICAN PULP FICTION ♦

LRH expedition is rightly remembered as conducting the first complete mineralogical survey of a Puerto Rico under United States jurisdiction.

There was many another adventure along this vein: As a lifetime member of the famed Explorers Club, L. Ron Hubbard charted North Pacific waters with the first shipboard radio direction finder, and so pioneered a long-range navigation system universally employed until the late twentieth century. While not to put too fine an edge on it, he also held a rare Master Mariner's license to pilot any vessel, of any tonnage in any ocean.

Yet lest we stray too far afield, there is an LRH note at this juncture in his saga, and it reads in part:

"I started out writing for the pulps, writing the best I knew, writing for every mag on the stands, slanting as well as I could."

To which one might add: His earliest submissions date from the summer of 1934, and included tales drawn from true-to-life Asian adventures, with characters roughly modeled on British/American intelligence operatives he had known in Shanghai. His early Westerns were similarly peppered with details drawn from personal experience. Although therein lay a first hard lesson from the often cruel world of the pulps. His first Westerns were soundly rejected as lacking the authenticity of a Max Brand yarn

Capt. L. Ron Hubbard in Ketchikan, Alaska, 1940, on his Alaskan Radio Experimental Expedition, the first of three voyages conducted under the Explorers Club flag.

(a particularly frustrating comment given L. Ron Hubbard's Westerns came straight from his Montana homeland, while Max Brand was a mediocre New York poet named Frederick Schiller Faust, who turned out implausible six-shooter tales from the terrace of an Italian villa).

Nevertheless, and needless to say, L. Ron Hubbard persevered and soon earned a reputation as among the most publishable names in pulp fiction, with a ninety percent placement rate of first-draft manuscripts. He was also among the most prolific, averaging between seventy and a hundred thousand words a month. Hence the rumors that L. Ron Hubbard had redesigned a typewriter for faster keyboard action and pounded out manuscripts on a continuous roll of butcher paper to save the precious seconds it took to insert a single sheet of paper into manual typewriters of the day.

That all L. Ron Hubbard stories did not run beneath said byline is yet another aspect of pulp fiction lore. That is, as publishers periodically rejected manuscripts from top-drawer authors if only to avoid paying top dollar, L. Ron Hubbard and company just as frequently replied with submissions under various pseudonyms. In Ron's case, the

> **A MAN OF MANY NAMES**
> *Between 1934 and 1950, L. Ron Hubbard authored more than fifteen million words of fiction in more than two hundred classic publications. To supply his fans and editors with stories across an array of genres and pulp titles, he adopted fifteen pseudonyms in addition to his already renowned L. Ron Hubbard byline.*
>
> Winchester Remington Colt
> Lt. Jonathan Daly
> Capt. Charles Gordon
> Capt. L. Ron Hubbard
> Bernard Hubbel
> Michael Keith
> Rene Lafayette
> Legionnaire 148
> Legionnaire 14830
> Ken Martin
> Scott Morgan
> Lt. Scott Morgan
> Kurt von Rachen
> Barry Randolph
> Capt. Humbert Reynolds

◆ AMERICAN PULP FICTION ◆

list included: Rene Lafayette, Captain Charles Gordon, Lt. Scott Morgan and the notorious Kurt von Rachen—supposedly on the lam for a murder rap, while hammering out two-fisted prose in Argentina. The point: While L. Ron Hubbard as Ken Martin spun stories of Southeast Asian intrigue, LRH as Barry Randolph authored tales of romance on the Western range—which, stretching between a dozen genres is how he came to stand among the two hundred elite authors providing close to a million tales through the glory days of American Pulp Fiction.

L. Ron Hubbard, circa 1930, at the outset of a literary career that would finally span half a century.

In evidence of exactly that, by 1936 L. Ron Hubbard was literally leading pulp fiction's elite as president of New York's American Fiction Guild. Members included a veritable pulp hall of fame: Lester "Doc Savage" Dent, Walter "The Shadow" Gibson, and the legendary Dashiell Hammett—to cite but a few.

Also in evidence of just where L. Ron Hubbard stood within his first two years on the American pulp circuit: By the spring of 1937, he was ensconced in Hollywood, adopting a Caribbean thriller for Columbia Pictures, remembered today as *The Secret of Treasure Island*. Comprising fifteen thirty-minute episodes, the L. Ron Hubbard screenplay led to the most profitable matinée serial in Hollywood history. In accord with Hollywood culture, he was thereafter continually called upon

• L. RON HUBBARD •

The 1937 Secret of Treasure Island, *a fifteen-episode serial adapted for the screen by L. Ron Hubbard from his novel,* Murder at Pirate Castle.

to rewrite/doctor scripts—most famously for long-time friend and fellow adventurer Clark Gable.

In the interim—and herein lies another distinctive chapter of the L. Ron Hubbard story—he continually worked to open Pulp Kingdom gates to up-and-coming authors. Or, for that matter, anyone who wished to write. It was a fairly unconventional stance, as markets were already thin and competition razor sharp. But the fact remains, it was an L. Ron Hubbard hallmark that he vehemently lobbied on behalf of young authors—regularly supplying instructional articles to trade journals, guest-lecturing to short story classes at George Washington University and Harvard, and even founding his own creative writing competition. It was established in 1940, dubbed the Golden Pen, and guaranteed winners both New York representation and publication in *Argosy*.

But it was John W. Campbell Jr.'s *Astounding Science Fiction* that finally proved the most memorable LRH vehicle. While every fan of L. Ron Hubbard's galactic epics undoubtedly knows the story, it nonetheless bears repeating: By late 1938, the pulp publishing magnate of Street & Smith was determined to revamp *Astounding Science Fiction* for broader readership. In particular, senior editorial director F. Orlin Tremaine called for stories with a stronger *human element*. When acting editor John W. Campbell balked, preferring his spaceship-driven tales, Tremaine enlisted Hubbard. Hubbard, in turn, replied with the genre's first truly *character-driven* works, wherein heroes are pitted not against bug-eyed monsters but the mystery and majesty of deep space itself—and thus was launched the Golden Age of Science Fiction.

The names alone are enough to quicken the pulse of any science fiction aficionado, including LRH friend and protégé, Robert Heinlein, Isaac Asimov, A. E. van Vogt and Ray Bradbury. Moreover, when coupled with LRH stories of fantasy, we further come to what's rightly been described as the foundation of every modern tale of horror: L. Ron Hubbard's immortal *Fear*. It was rightly proclaimed by Stephen King as one of the very few works to genuinely warrant that overworked term "classic"—as in: *"This is a classic tale of creeping, surreal menace and horror.... This is one of the really, really good ones."*

To accommodate the greater body of L. Ron Hubbard fantasies, Street & Smith inaugurated *Unknown*—a classic pulp if there ever was one, and wherein readers were soon thrilling to the likes of *Typewriter in the Sky* and *Slaves of Sleep* of which Frederik Pohl would declare: *"There are bits and pieces from Ron's work that became part of the language in ways that very few other writers managed."*

And, indeed, at J. W. Campbell Jr.'s insistence, Ron was regularly drawing on themes from the Arabian Nights and

L. Ron Hubbard, 1948, among fellow science fiction luminaries at the World Science Fiction Convention in Toronto.

• L. RON HUBBARD •

so introducing readers to a world of genies, jinn, Aladdin and Sinbad—all of which, of course, continue to float through cultural mythology to this day.

At least as influential in terms of post-apocalypse stories was L. Ron Hubbard's 1940 *Final Blackout*. Generally acclaimed as the finest anti-war novel of the decade and among the ten best works of the genre ever authored—here, too, was a tale that would live on in ways few other writers imagined.

Portland, Oregon, 1943; L. Ron Hubbard, captain of the US Navy subchaser PC 815.

Hence, the later Robert Heinlein verdict: "Final Blackout *is as perfect a piece of science fiction as has ever been written.*"

Like many another who both lived and wrote American pulp adventure, the war proved a tragic end to Ron's sojourn in the pulps. He served with distinction in four theaters and was highly decorated for commanding corvettes in the North Pacific. He was also grievously wounded in combat, lost many a close friend and colleague and thus resolved to say farewell to pulp fiction and devote himself to what it had supported these many years—namely, his serious research.

But in no way was the LRH literary saga at an end, for as he wrote some thirty years later, in 1980:

"Recently there came a period when I had little to do. This was novel in a life so crammed with busy years, and I decided to amuse myself by writing a novel that was pure *science fiction*."

That work was *Battlefield Earth: A Saga of the Year 3000*. It was an immediate *New York Times* bestseller and, in fact, the first international science fiction blockbuster in decades. It was not, however, L. Ron Hubbard's magnum opus, as that distinction is generally reserved for his next and final work: The 1.2 million word *Mission Earth*.

> **Final Blackout** *is as perfect a piece of science fiction as has ever been written.*
> —Robert Heinlein

How he managed those 1.2 million words in just over twelve months is yet another piece of the L. Ron Hubbard legend. But the fact remains, he did indeed author a ten-volume *dekalogy* that lives in publishing history for the fact that each and every volume of the series was also a *New York Times* bestseller.

Moreover, as subsequent generations discovered L. Ron Hubbard through republished works and novelizations of his screenplays, the mere fact of his name on a cover signaled an international bestseller. . . . Until, to date, sales of his works exceed hundreds of millions, and he otherwise remains among the most enduring and widely read authors in literary history. Although as a final word on the tales of L. Ron Hubbard, perhaps it's enough to simply reiterate what editors told readers in the glory days of American Pulp Fiction:

He writes the way he does, brothers, because he's been there, seen it and done it!

THE STORIES FROM THE GOLDEN AGE

Your ticket to adventure starts here with the Stories from the Golden Age collection by master storyteller L. Ron Hubbard. These gripping tales are set in a kaleidoscope of exotic locales and brim with fascinating characters, including some of the most vile villains, dangerous dames and brazen heroes you'll ever get to meet.

The entire collection of over one hundred and fifty stories is being released in a series of eighty books and audiobooks. For an up-to-date listing of available titles, go to www.goldenagestories.com.

AIR ADVENTURE

Arctic Wings
The Battling Pilot
Boomerang Bomber
The Crate Killer
The Dive Bomber
Forbidden Gold
Hurtling Wings
The Lieutenant Takes the Sky

Man-Killers of the Air
On Blazing Wings
Red Death Over China
Sabotage in the Sky
Sky Birds Dare!
The Sky-Crasher
Trouble on His Wings
Wings Over Ethiopia

• STORIES FROM THE GOLDEN AGE •

FAR-FLUNG ADVENTURE

The Adventure of "X" Hurricane
All Frontiers Are Jealous The Iron Duke
The Barbarians Machine Gun 21,000
The Black Sultan Medals for Mahoney
Black Towers to Danger Price of a Hat
The Bold Dare All Red Sand
Buckley Plays a Hunch The Sky Devil
The Cossack The Small Boss of Nunaloha
Destiny's Drum The Squad That Never Came Back
Escape for Three Starch and Stripes
Fifty-Fifty O'Brien Tomb of the Ten Thousand Dead
The Headhunters Trick Soldier
Hell's Legionnaire While Bugles Blow!
He Walked to War Yukon Madness
Hostage to Death

SEA ADVENTURE

Cargo of Coffins The Phantom Patrol
The Drowned City Sea Fangs
False Cargo Submarine
Grounded Twenty Fathoms Down
Loot of the Shanung Under the Black Ensign
Mister Tidwell, Gunner

• STORIES FROM THE GOLDEN AGE •

TALES FROM THE ORIENT

The Devil—With Wings
The Falcon Killer
Five Mex for a Million
Golden Hell
The Green God
Hurricane's Roar
Inky Odds
Orders Is Orders

Pearl Pirate
The Red Dragon
Spy Killer
Tah
The Trail of the Red Diamonds
Wind-Gone-Mad
Yellow Loot

MYSTERY

The Blow Torch Murder
Brass Keys to Murder
Calling Squad Cars!
The Carnival of Death
The Chee-Chalker
Dead Men Kill
The Death Flyer
Flame City

The Grease Spot
Killer Ape
Killer's Law
The Mad Dog Murder
Mouthpiece
Murder Afloat
The Slickers
They Killed Him Dead

• STORIES FROM THE GOLDEN AGE •

FANTASY

Borrowed Glory *If I Were You*
The Crossroads *The Last Drop*
Danger in the Dark *The Room*
The Devil's Rescue *The Tramp*
He Didn't Like Cats

SCIENCE FICTION

The Automagic Horse *A Matter of Matter*
Battle of Wizards *The Obsolete Weapon*
Battling Bolto *One Was Stubborn*
The Beast *The Planet Makers*
Beyond All Weapons *The Professor Was a Thief*
A Can of Vacuum *The Slaver*
The Conroy Diary *Space Can*
The Dangerous Dimension *Strain*
Final Enemy *Tough Old Man*
The Great Secret *240,000 Miles Straight Up*
Greed *When Shadows Fall*
The Invaders

• STORIES FROM THE GOLDEN AGE •

WESTERN

The Baron of Coyote River
Blood on His Spurs
Boss of the Lazy B
Branded Outlaw
Cattle King for a Day
Come and Get It
Death Waits at Sundown
Devil's Manhunt
The Ghost Town Gun-Ghost
Gun Boss of Tumbleweed
Gunman!
Gunman's Tally
The Gunner from Gehenna
Hoss Tamer
Johnny, the Town Tamer
King of the Gunmen
The Magic Quirt
Man for Breakfast
The No-Gun Gunhawk
The No-Gun Man
The Ranch That No One Would Buy
Reign of the Gila Monster
Ride 'Em, Cowboy
Ruin at Rio Piedras
Shadows from Boot Hill
Silent Pards
Six-Gun Caballero
Stacked Bullets
Stranger in Town
Tinhorn's Daughter
The Toughest Ranger
Under the Diehard Brand
Vengeance Is Mine!
When Gilhooly Was in Flower

Your Next Ticket to Adventure

Launch into Adventure in the Perilous Skies!

Pilot Terry Lee has taught Bill Trevillian everything he knows about flying, enough that Bill's now considered the ace of American test pilots just as war breaks out in World War II Europe. Unknown to Bill, Terry's also taught his own kid sister, Kip, who's now almost as good a pilot as Bill and quite the looker to boot.

When France and Great Britain must choose between different American plane designs to outfly the newest and deadliest Nazi fighters, the competing companies send their two best test pilots . . . Kip and Bill. Unfortunately, a spy also has been sent to infiltrate and sabotage the planes to make sure that neither the French nor British will consider them safe enough to fly. Soon Kip and Bill suspect the other of sabotage—a problem that not only threatens their already electric relationship but their very lives.

Get
Sabotage in the Sky

Paperback or Audiobook: $9.95 each
Free Shipping & Handling for Book Club Members
Call toll-free: 1-877-8GALAXY (1-877-842-5299)
or go online to **www.goldenagestories.com**

Galaxy Press, 7051 Hollywood Blvd., Suite 200, Hollywood, CA 90028

JOIN THE PULP REVIVAL
America in the 1930s and 40s

P ulp fiction was in its heyday and 30 million readers were regularly riveted by the larger-than-life tales of master storyteller L. Ron Hubbard. For this was pulp fiction's golden age, when the writing was raw and every page packed a walloping punch.

That magic can now be yours. An evocative world of nefarious villains, exotic intrigues, courageous heroes and heroines—a world that today's cinema has barely tapped for tales of adventure and swashbucklers.

Enroll today in the Stories from the Golden Age Club and begin receiving your monthly feature edition selected from more than 150 stories in the collection.

You may choose to enjoy them as either a paperback or audiobook for the special membership price of $9.95 each month along with FREE shipping and handling.

CALL TOLL-FREE: **1-877-8GALAXY**
(1-877-842-5299) OR GO ONLINE TO
www.goldenagestories.com
AND BECOME PART OF THE PULP REVIVAL!

Prices are set in US dollars only. For non-US residents, please call
1-323-466-7815 for pricing information. Free shipping available for US residents only.

Galaxy Press, 7051 Hollywood Blvd., Suite 200, Hollywood, CA 90028